THE CASE OF THE
VANISHING VENTRILOQUIST

By the Same Author

The Case of the Vanishing Ventriloquist

A McGURK MYSTERY

BY E. W. HILDICK
Illustrated by Kathy Parkinson

MACMILLAN PUBLISHING COMPANY
New York

To Margi Lu, K. T., and J. B.
of the P. I. Agency

Macmillan Publishing Company
866 Third Avenue, New York, N.Y. 10022
Collier Macmillan Canada, Inc.
Printed in the United States of America

10 9 8 7 6 5 4 3 2 1

Library of Congress Cataloging in Publication Data
Hildick, E. W. (Edmund Wallace), date.
The case of the vanishing ventriloquist.
Summary: The McGurk organization must act to prevent
a crime—but they don't know what the crime will be.
1. Children's stories, American.   [1. Mystery and
detective stories]   1. Parkinson, Kathy, ill.
II. Title.   III. Series.
PZ7.H5463Cavm 1985   [Fic]   84-21801
ISBN 0-02-743930-5

CONTENTS

1 New Member?

"What's keeping Wanda?"

I don't think I've ever seen McGurk look as tense and impatient as he did that morning.

He was sitting in the rocking chair at the head of the table in the basement at his house—our headquarters. In front of him was a bunch of papers. He was keeping them covered with his hands, but I could see part of the heading on the top paper. Even from where I was sitting, I could recognize his curly handwriting. Even upside down.

But that was all I could make out: *The McGurk Organization Annual Prom—* and I was dying to know what the rest of that last word was.

I was thinking that surely it couldn't be Prom-*enade*? McGurk gets some really weird ideas, but I couldn't figure him arranging an annual *dance*!

"She'll be here soon, McGurk," I said. "Meanwhile, what's that bunch of papers about? You might as well be giving us a few background details."

"No!" Now his fingers covered the rest of the heading. "This is too important to announce in bits and pieces. That's why I said for everybody to be here at nine-thirty *sharp*." He glared at the door. "What's keeping her?"

Brains Bellingham took off his glasses and gave them a polish. He was sitting next to me. He, too, had been peering hard at that heading. So hard that his eyes were watering.

"Her visitor, I guess," he said. "McGurk, does this meeting have something to do with—?"

"What visitor?" snapped McGurk.

"Japanese visitor," said Brains.

"Her pen pal from Japan," I said.

"Yeah!" said Willie Sandowsky. "She's been talking about it for weeks."

McGurk glared at him.

"Yeah, yeah! I know! But *already*? I thought the kid wasn't coming until the *end* of July?"

The rest of us looked at one another. Was McGurk losing his marbles?

I coughed politely.

"Uh—it *is* the end of July, McGurk."

He blinked. Then glanced down.

"Yeah—well—I've been busy these last few days." He scowled at me. "I thought I told you to tell her this was an *extra-special* meeting?"

"Sure, but—" I turned to the door. "Anyway, here she—"

I'd been going to say, "Here she is." But that was no longer correct. The "she" was now "they." Wanda had with her this little Japanese kid.

And when I saw *that*, I just sat tight and braced myself for the explosion.

"Sorry we're late, McGurk," said Wanda, with a calm placid smile.

She had a reassuring hand on the kid's shoulder, like she knew there might be a ruckus. But the smile was too calm. It gave away the fact that Wanda couldn't have been thinking clearly. The look on McGurk's face should have warned her.

As for the Japanese girl, she, too, was wearing a calm placid smile. Maybe Wanda had caught it off *her*. The visitor had only arrived the previous evening, but I guess girls get to know each other a lot quicker than guys do. Let a couple of girls share a bedroom for just one night and they get up in the morning as close as sisters.

That smile was the only thing they did look alike in, though.

Wanda is quite tall for a girl just going on twelve, and she has long dusty-looking blond hair. The visitor was very small, even though nearly the same age. In fact she was a lot smaller than Brains. And her hair was neat and thick and shiny and black. It was made to look even blacker by a white headband. There was some Japanese writing in red on it, and that writing was repeated on her white T-shirt.

I also had time to note a few more details—because the explosion hadn't occurred yet. Details like the crisp new denim shorts and spotless white socks and sneakers.

And the doll.

The doll was like a replica of the kid. T-shirt, headband, shorts and all. Except it wasn't the usual kind of doll. It was partly a glove puppet. The girl had one hand stuffed inside it and was making it look around at each of us in turn.

Maybe that's what postponed the explosion.

McGurk was staring at it with disgust and fascination.

Then he gave his head a shake.

"What do you mean—*we*—Officer Grieg? Sorry *we're* late?"

"Mari and I."

Wanda was still wearing the calm sweet smile. She gave her friend's shoulder an encouraging pat. But even the doll flinched when McGurk roared:

"You don't have to apologize for *her*! She wasn't *invited*! Why are *you* late?"

Wanda's smile trembled slightly. But there was a glint in her eyes. She gave her head a toss. Then, calm again, she said:

"Because Mari wasn't quite ready. She couldn't

make up her mind which doll to bring along." She turned. "Mari, I'd like you to meet the rest of the McGurk Organization. The one who's been doing all the talking—"

"No, no, please!" said Mari. "Let me see if I can guess, from your letter descriptions."

Now if those two girls had sat up all night figuring out ways to get McGurk to simmer down, they couldn't have hit on a better one.

I mean, this guessing who we were from our descriptions was pure detective work, testing Wanda's accuracy and Mari's observation.

I won't say McGurk stopped looking annoyed. But at least he relaxed enough to sit back and rock gently.

"Go on, then," he grunted. "Make it snappy."

"Thank you," said Mari. "First allow me to say my own name. Mari Yoshimura, from Osaka, in Japan. My pen pal, Wanda Grieg—"

"We know *her*!" said McGurk. "Now you tell us who the *rest* of us are."

Mari nodded slightly. She smiled at McGurk.

"You, of course, are McGurk. Jack P. McGurk, Head of famous McGurk Organization, Detectives. Even without hearing you speak, I would know from hair—red. And from freckles around nose—numerous. And eyes—green. But"—Mari frowned and glanced up at Wanda—"he is more handsome than in your letters."

McGurk had started to smirk from the word *famous* onward. At the mention of *handsome* his smirk broadened.

Then suddenly he glared at Wanda.

"Hey! What *did* you write about me?"

But Mari and her doll had turned to the other end of the table.

"The second one I recognize easily is *you* one," she said to Willie (making one of her rare slips in the English language). "Willie Sandowsky?"

Willie was blushing. He looked really pleased. Luckily, he didn't ask her why she recognized him. I'm sure Mari would have been much too polite to tell him it was because of the length of his nose. Which I bet it was.

"You have the wonderful and delicate sense of smell. By using that sense, you have solved many cases."

Willie nodded happily. And as Mari went on to mention some of those cases, I half expected Mc-Gurk to chip in.

But he kept quiet. While Mari and Wanda were turned toward Willie, McGurk was doing something very strange.

Winking at me and Brains, he very quietly

reached forward and moved my typewriter so that it was in front of Brains.

"Hey!" I gasped—but he frowned at me to be quiet.

"Okay, Mari," he said. "You've shown how smart you are at recognizing people from their descriptions when it's easy. Like me with my red hair. And Officer Sandowsky with his long thin—uh—legs. So now come back up here and tell us who this officer is with the glasses and the typewriter."

Well, the nerve of that guy! Both Brains and I wear glasses. So putting the typewriter in front of Brains was a real cunning move—more suitable for a con man than a detective.

Wanda must have thought so too. The calm smile vanished.

"Just a second, McGurk—!"

"Ah-ah! No coaching, Officer Grieg!"

There was a long pause. Mari looked puzzled. She kept glancing from the typewriter to Brains. Then she'd take a peek at me.

And as she did this, I'm darned if the doll didn't keep doing the same!

Then it put its mouth to Mari's ear, and I could have sworn I heard it whispering.

Mari's face lit up. Her brown eyes sparkled.

She turned to me.

"Ah, so! The typewriter must be broken, Joey. Yes?"

"Uh—I—"

"You *are* Joey Rockaway? With dark hair, glasses and intelligent face. Yes. So because typewriter is broken you give it to Brains—real name Gerald— Gerald Bellingham. Because he is science expert and good to repairing mechanical things. Correct?"

"Well—not exactly." Now *I* was blushing. "I mean it isn't broken, Mari. But yes—I am Joey Rockaway. I keep the records and write about the cases we solve."

Mari was nodding. She turned to our science expert.

"I would recognize Brains also—may I call you Brains, dear sir?"

"Sure!"

Brains was grinning, enjoying the look on Mc-Gurk's face. After all, the Big Leader himself hadn't been addressed as "sir"!

"I would recognize you also from your short, bristling, fair hair and because you are little. What was word in your letters, Wanda? Little *squirt*—no?"

So it became Wanda's turn to blush.

"Uh—no! I mean—you mustn't say that word, Mari. It isn't polite."

Brains was soon smirking again as Mari, looking grave, continued:

"I am so very sorry! I did not mean to be impolite, Gerald, truly. My father, he owns electronics corporation and I know how smart and uh—not-squirt one must be to understand electronics things. Like you and he."

Brains gaped.

"Hey! Wait! What did you say your name is? Yoshimura? Mari *Yoshimura*? Hey, your father—he isn't the head of *Yoshimura Electronics*?"

"Yes. Is not very big firm but—"

"Aw, come on! It is only just about *the* best!" Brains had to break off to wipe his glasses. "Hey! Wow! Is Mr. Yoshimura—is your father staying at the Griegs', too?"

Mari shook her head.

"No. He and my mother left this morning to take trip to Chicago and other cities. On business. But what are *you* working on, Brains? I told my father some things about you in Wanda's letters. And he say, 'Keep eyes on that young man, Mari. He sounds very smart. Very smart indeed!' "

"Well, gee! Tell him I'm busy right now working on a special midget cordless telephone. One that

kids would be able to afford and use in emergencies. Right now I have a problem with—"

"Right *now*, Officer Bellingham, you are attending a special meeting of the McGurk Organization." Our leader's green eyes were flashing. "And right *now* you are wasting the Organization's time." He glanced again at the bunch of papers. "Officer Grieg, I'll give you ten minutes to take Miss Whatsername back to your house and leave her to play with her dolls. Then I want you back here, ready to—"

"Excuse *me*, McGurk—" Wanda's glassy smile had returned. "Mari has something very special to show you. . . . Show him, Mari."

Mari gave that little nod, then took her hand out of the back of the doll and held out a folded card.

McGurk scowled.

"What is it?"

"My ID card," said Mari. "Please examine."

"Your ID card!" scoffed McGurk. He leered at us over the top of it. "And what Organization do *you* belong to, Mari? The Doll Collectors of Japan, Incorporated? Heh! heh!" Then he froze in mid-chuckle. The grin went into a nose dive. *"Hey!"* he howled. "Whose idea was *this*?"

By then I'd had time to see what was typed on the front.

This:

```
Honaorary Temporary  Maember
             of
  The MacGurk Organization
```

2 Mari Shows Her Skill

The card was a copy of our own. It had the same spaces and headings for such things as photograph, fingerprints, height and so on.

And I could tell this at a glance because I'm the guy who designed and did the typing for our cards.

I began to feel just a little miffed.

"You might have asked *me* to make out the card," I said to Wanda. "And if you couldn't wait, you might have made a better job of the typing."

"Who says *I* made out the card? And anyway, why shouldn't I—?"

"Silence!" roared McGurk. "Or I'll suspend you both from duty!" He turned to Mari. "I'm sorry, but I'll have to confiscate this."

"But—but—"

"It isn't your fault, I know. But you shouldn't have let her talk you into committing an offense."

"Please?" said Mari, looking bewildered.

"*Offense?*" howled Wanda.

McGurk smiled grimly.

"Yeah. Offense. See what it says here? *Officer's Name: Mari Yoshimura.* Well, that's the offense. Impersonating an officer of the Organization." He turned to Mari. "Very serious! But we'll overlook it this one time, seeing how you're new to the country."

"Oh, boy!" groaned Wanda, flinging her hair about. "Will you listen to the guy!" Then she forced the smile back. "McGurk," she said, "don't you have any feeling for a guest at all?"

"Sure—*my* guests."

"But Mari is the guest of us all. An honored guest who's come all this way to visit the Organization she's heard so much about."

"You're breaking my heart!" said McGurk, looking a shade uneasy.

Wanda's smile broadened. I guess she sensed she was getting him all softened up.

"So is it too much to ask for this very fine, very smart young visitor to be allowed to become a temporary member? Just for the duration of her stay?"

"Huh! This isn't just any old club. Now if she was *detective* smart—"

"But she is!" said Wanda. "Show him, Mari! Do it! Show him the 'How To Deal with Menacing Strangers' routine."

"Now?" said Mari.

"Right now! Just the way you showed me last night."

Mari nodded.

"Very well. . . . You ready?" she said to the doll.

The doll nodded.

"Whenever you are!" it replied.

Well, this was a double whammy. The name of the routine had already silenced the rest of us, McGurk included. But when that doll spoke back—in a strange little piping but very clear voice—we just gaped.

"Now, little girl," said Mari, "let me ask you something."

"Sure!" said the doll. "Anything you like."

By now I was watching Mari's face carefully. And I could swear her lips hardly moved. Not until she replied:

"Very well. Tell me—do you like candies?"

The doll quivered and made yummy lip-smacking noises.

"Do I like candies? Does Mr. McGurk like solving

cases? Of course I like candies. Don't ask stupid questions!"

"Heh! heh! Good kid!"

The remark came from McGurk, flushed at the respectful mention of his name. Wanda raised her eyebrows at me and grinned.

Mari's face remained very serious as she stared at the doll.

"Very well. So what do you say if a strange adult offers you candies in the street?"

The doll's right hand shot out eagerly, as if to

accept. Then its left hand gave the right hand a loud smack and the doll drew back, shaking its head.

"I say to stranger—*'Get lost!'* "

Willie cackled. McGurk guffawed. Brains giggled.

"No, no, *no!*" Mari said to the doll. "You must always be polite. Now—*what* do you say if strange adult offers you candies?"

"I say—uh—'Get lost, *sir!*' "

I thought Willie was going to be sick, laughing.

"No, no, no!" said Mari, sternly.

" 'Get lost—*ma'am?*' "

"Not *get lost* at all, you silly child! You say, 'No, thank you.' Say it!"

"No, thank you!"

"That's good. Then what?"

"I walk away."

The doll turned and began to walk with its head in the air.

"Yes, good. But wait. What do you do if person follows and keeps offering candies?"

The doll stopped. It lowered its head like it was thinking. Then, with a swiftness that made Brains jump, it turned and aimed a punch at Mari's nose.

"I punch him! Like that! On the nose!"

"No, no, no!"

"On *chin* then!"

"No! You must *never* do that. He may get angry and hurt you."

The doll dipped its head again, then looked up.

"I call policeman!"

"Very good!" said Mari.

"The best thing you can do, kid!" said McGurk, looking at the doll like it was *alive!*

"You bet!" said Willie.

"Shush!" said Brains, seeing Mari hadn't finished.

"But if there is no policeman around, little girl?"

"I go to nearest adults. And I say, 'This person is bothering me. Please tell him stop.' "

Then Mari bowed and the doll bowed and we all clapped—including McGurk.

"Well, McGurk?" said Wanda.

"Well—yeah—terrific, Mari! Real good!" Then he shook his head. "But really that's crime prevention work. Not detection."

Wanda groaned.

"McGurk! Crime prevention is just as important as detection. You know that!"

"Yes, but—well—"

"The police department has a crime prevention unit," said Brains. "Why shouldn't we?"

"Yeah!" said Willie.

"It makes sense," I said. "We could get Mari to

tour the neighborhood, doing her act for all the little kids."

"Part of the McGurk Organization's service to the community," said Brains.

McGurk's eyes started to gleam at this. Then he sighed and shook his head again.

"I'm sorry," he said. "Any other time, but not this next couple of weeks. They're too important."

"What do you mean?" said Wanda. "What's so important about them?"

"Everything's important about them, Officer Grieg. Organizationwise."

"Why? We don't have a case, do we?"

"No," said McGurk. "But in a way it's even *more* important."

We stared at him. If anyone had asked me one minute earlier, I'd have said that to McGurk *nothing* could be more important than a case. But *nothing*!

"Come on, McGurk!" I said.

"Be serious!" said Brains.

"I was never more serious in my life," said McGurk, picking up that bunch of papers.

3 McGurk Springs His Big Surprise

McGurk turned to Mari.

"Sorry," he said. "But this is strictly an Organization affair. Why don't you go back to the Grieg house and practice your routine? That's a really good act, Mari. And maybe the next time you visit—"

"If *she* goes, I go!" said Wanda.

McGurk shrugged.

"Suit yourself. I can let you have two weeks' leave. It's your privilege, Officer Grieg."

Wanda looked taken aback. And puzzled. And suspicious.

"Well—uh—sure! If that's all right by *you*, McGurk?"

"Sure. No problem." He paused. "It just means

you'll miss out on the Organization's Annual Promotion Exam, that's all."

I gave a start.

"Annual *what*, McGurk?"

"*Exam?*" gasped Willie.

"*Promotion?*" whispered Brains.

McGurk was now wearing his most obnoxious smirk.

"Sure! I've decided it's time to promote one of you to the rank of Lieutenant and another to Sergeant. And since you've all got your own expert skills, I figured the only way to promote you is on your *all-around* detective ability. So I worked out these tests."

He gave the bunch of papers a gentle riffle.

Well!

Everyone was knocked for a loop.

I, Joey Rockaway, expert in words, just couldn't find any to express *my* surprise.

Wanda, always ready with some snappy retort, was the same.

Brains was polishing his glasses like mad.

Willie rubbed his nose like *that* needed polishing.

And even Mari was impressed.

"Excuse me," she said gravely. "I will go now. I am sorry to delay start. I know how important examinations are. In Japan they are *very* important."

"But—"

"Please, Wanda!" Mari held up her free hand. "I can do like Chief McGurk says and practice with dolls. Truly! You *must* stay and compete in your examination. You must *not* lose opportunity for promotion."

This was very sad, but I think we all began to breathe a little easier when we realized how well Mari was taking it.

"She's right, Wanda," said Brains. "I'll still whip you in the tests—but I'd like the chance to *prove* it."

"Oh yeah?" said Wanda.

"Sure!" said Willie. "You stay, Wanda! See if you can't beat Brains and get yourself made Sergeant."

"Hey!" I said. "Don't be so modest, Willie! You could still make Sergeant yourself."

"Nuh-huh!" Willie grinned. "*I'm* going to make Lieutenant!"

Then Wanda said, "But surely, McGurk, these tests won't last two weeks? I mean, we won't be sitting down all day every day for two—?"

"They are *not* sitting-down written tests, Officer Grieg. They are practical tests. Out there in the streets. A whole bunch of them. Anyway," he continued, "*nobody's* going to be promoted if we don't make a start." He turned to Mari. "By the way, before you go, what do those words mean? On your shirt and that head thing?"

I shoved my notebook toward him, to show him where I'd already made a copy of those letters.

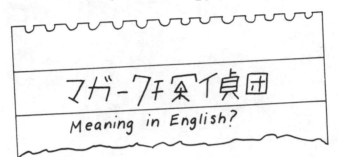

Meaning in English?

"As word expert, *I* was going to ask her that," I said.

McGurk nodded. He looked pleased.

"Good work, Officer Rockaway. Glad to see you keep on your toes at all times. But has he copied it *correctly*, Mari?"

Mari took a look and nodded, sad faced. There was a small teardrop glistening in each of her eyes.

"Yes. Very good, Joey."

"So what does it mean, Mari?"

She shrugged.

"Oh—nothing important. It—it just doesn't mean anything—now."

The teardrops grew bigger. I didn't like to press for an answer. She was walking to the door anyway.

When she got there she turned—smiling again.

"Have good examinations! Hope you *all* get top marks!"

Then she walked out.

"Excuse me, McGurk," said Wanda (and now *her* eyes were glistening). "I'll just make sure she gets home okay. I'll be right back."

"Hurry it up then!" he said gruffly.

Now, McGurk is always very fair.

So while Wanda was out, he refused to give us any details about the tests.

"You'll all begin with the same chance," he said. "Nobody gets a head start in *this* exam."

After that, all we could do was sit around and say what a shame it was that Mari had to come at such a time.

"I could have got her to ask her father for his advice on my electronics experiments," said Brains.

"Yeah!" said Willie. "And I could have asked her about artificial smells."

"Huh?"

"Sure! There's a factory in Japan that makes all kinds of *special* artificial perfumes. Not just flower smells. It was on TV once."

I sighed.

"And I'd have loved to learn some of the language. Especially the writing."

"And I wouldn't have minded asking about—"

But what aspect of Japanese life McGurk would have been interested to check on he didn't get around to saying, because just then Wanda returned.

Her eyes were still glistening—but in a much more purposeful way.

"Okay, McGurk. Mari's feeling a lot better now. So let's get with the tests, huh? The sooner we do, the sooner the McGurk Organization will start catching up with the times."

"Oh?"

"Sure!" said Wanda. "By having its first-ever girl lieutenant!"

Please— hold the paper this week

4 McGurk's Scoresheet

McGurk wasn't fooling when he said he'd been busy. He'd worked out no fewer than six tests.

"Each one deals with a different detective skill," he explained. "Like the first one." He began to read from the top paper. " 'Skill at Spotting Things That Invite Crime and Criminals.' "

Willie gaped. "What things?"

"Giveaway signs," I said. "Like notes pinned to front doors, telling everyone there's nobody home. Right, McGurk?"

McGurk nodded.

"That's just one example, yes." He looked around.

"And the first test is for you all to go out searching for such signs. *Anything* that makes it easier for crooks. And make a note of each one. Okay?"

A murmur of approval went up. I could tell that everyone there had started to get ideas already.

"How long do we have?" asked Brains, briskly.

"All the rest of today and part of tomorrow morning," said McGurk. "All night, if you like. So long as you're here with your lists at nine-thirty sharp in the morning. Then I'll tell you what marks you'll get."

"*How* will you mark them?" asked Wanda.

"One for each genuine sign," said McGurk.

"How many of these signs do we need to spot?" said Willie. "To get top marks?"

McGurk smiled craftily.

"As many as you can, Officer Sandowsky. That's the beauty of the McGurk Detective Aptitude Tests. The more examples you collect, the more you score."

"Does this go for all the tests?" asked Brains.

"Yes. Then, at the end, all the marks will be added up. And the one who gets most will be made Lieutenant. And the second will be made Sergeant. I've worked out a scoresheet, which I'll pin up."

He held up one of the pieces of paper See the top of the next page for a copy of it.

NAME OF OFFICER	MARKS					
	Test #1	Test #2	Test #3	Test #4	Test #5	Test #6
BELLINGHAM						
GRIEG						
ROCKAWAY						
SANDOWSKY						

"You'll see the names are in alphabetical order," said McGurk.

"That's okay!" said Brains, smirking. "That's where my name will *still* be at the end. On top! How d'you spell *Lieutenant* Bellingham, Joey?"

I frowned. Brains can be even more obnoxious than McGurk at times.

"What are the subjects of the other tests, McGurk?" I asked.

"Ah-ah! One test at a time, Officer Rockaway! Any more questions?"

Wanda had been looking a lot happier.

"Yes," she said. "We split up for this, right?"

"Sure!" said McGurk. "How else? You don't want

any of the others to see what you've spotted—what they might have missed themselves—do you?"

"No way!" said Wanda. "But there's no reason why Mari shouldn't tag along with me, is there?"

"I object!" cried Brains, getting up and banging the table like a TV lawyer. "Mari would help her spot more than she would on her own!"

"Yeah!" said Willie.

"Two heads are better than one," I said. "Very unfair!"

"It wouldn't be *fair*," said Wanda, "if I could only spend one measly hour on *my* test, while you guys had all the time in the world!"

"How d'you mean?" said McGurk.

"Well I can't just leave Mari for the rest of the day, can I? She's my guest."

"I still object!" said Brains. "There's nothing to—"

"*Silence!*" roared McGurk, thumping the table like he was a TV *judge*. He turned. "You have a point there, Officer Grieg. So—raise your right hand."

"Huh?"

"Raise your right hand! . . . Now. Do you solemnly swear, on your word of honor, that you won't get Mari to help you?"

"Yes!" said Wanda. "And I'll do better than that!" She held her head back and half closed her eyes. "May I never climb another tree for the rest of my life if I don't keep my word!"

There was a deep silence. I mean, tree climbing is Wanda's one great hobby. It may seem strange, for a girl. But it's true.

McGurk was impressed.

"Okay," he said. "That's good enough for me. Besides," he went on, looking beady eyed again, "I'll be out there making my own tour. Checking on you all. Making sure none of you cheat by *inventing* examples."

Willie looked shocked.

"We wouldn't do that, McGurk! Why—uh"—he raised *his* right hand—"*may I lose my sense of smell forever if I do that!*"

"And may *I* never write another word!" I said.

Then Brains stood up, took off his glasses, closed his eyes tight, raised his right hand, and said:

"*May all my experiments go wrong if I do so cheat!*"

And although he didn't know it at the time, Brains's oath turned out to be the spookiest of all.

5 The First Test

During the rest of the day, the McGurk Organization was scattered. To outsiders, it must have looked like we'd had a big split-up, with everybody deciding to work alone—snooping around houses, parking lots, supermarkets and so on, with notebooks ready.

Quite often we'd run into one another. Like for instance in the residential streets. It being July, a lot of people were on vacation. This meant that a certain number of them would be sure to do dumb things. On the opposite page, there's a bunch of examples I collected in the first half hour.

All the members of the Organization were wise to *that* sort of thing.

When we did bump into one another, any person not knowing about the test would have been sure we'd had a big row before splitting up. They'd have guessed this from the way we'd frown at each other, then hurry away without speaking. With McGurk himself popping up everywhere and scowling at us.

"Don't look so *ugly*, McGurk!" I said, when he surprised me by emerging from the bushes at the side of the Gerhardi house. "You make me feel all guilty when I've done nothing wrong!"

TEST # 1

CRIME - INVITING SIGNS

Jones House, E.Beech St.
Grass on front lawn left
to grow too tall.

Parker House, E. Beech
mailbox overflowing.

Gerhardi House, E. Olive.
3-days' newspapers left
unopened on front porch.

"That's okay, Officer Rockaway. I'm only doing my duty, watching out for any monkey business in my department. Figure me as one of those internal affairs cops you see on TV."

"Yeah!" I said, still miffed. "The ones the others call shoo-flies!"

By midafternoon, though, I was feeling very pleased. Already, I'd noted ten items in the neighborhood area, including two cars left parked with the keys in the ignition. Now I was all set to rack up another ten or so downtown.

And I was just going to make a start in the supermarket parking lot when I ran into Wanda and Mari.

I hadn't noticed them in the neighborhood streets, so I was *very* alert when I saw that not only did Wanda have a notebook, *but so did Mari!*

"What's with *you*, Joey?" said Wanda, quickly closing her notebook.

"I see Mari has a notebook, too," I said.

"Good afternoon, Joey!" said Mari.

She was smiling politely. I noticed she was no longer wearing the T-shirt and headband with the writing on them. She'd changed these for plain, light blue ones.

"Does McGurk know about this?" I said to Wanda. "Mari also making notes?"

"As a matter of fact, yes," said Wanda. "So? Is there any law against Mari making her own list? Just for her own interest and amusement?"

"No. But—"

"I do not tell Wanda what I see," said Mari, looking rather hurt. Then her expression became very grave. "May I never be able to talk my dolls again if I do!" she added, raising her right hand.

No doubt this had impressed McGurk. But I could see another danger here.

"Well?" said Wanda. "Feel better now?"

"About your honesty, yes," I said. "But I really don't see how you can both be scribbling away, side by side, all day, without your *accidentally* catching a peek at what Mari's been writing."

"True!" said Wanda, with the calm smile again. "Very true! In fact I *do* keep catching a peek. Quite by accident, of course." Then her smile became broader and far less ladylike. "And a lot of good it does me! Show him, Mari!"

Mari held up her book, opened.

The page was full of tiny, neat, Japanese writing.

Both girls started laughing—Mari like a tinkling fountain, Wanda like a splashing faucet.

I frowned at the faucet. "You sure you can't read Japanese?"

"Yes. Can *you*, Mr. Word Expert?"

"No. I guess—"

"Well then! Now if you don't mind, we'd like to get on with the test!"

All the members of the Organization turned up promptly the following morning.

"Right, men. I'll check your lists," said McGurk. "Starting with yours, Officer Bellingham."

I was glad to see Brains had filled only three or

four notebook pages. My own list ran to six. But then I remembered his writing was pretty small, and I was in a sweat while McGurk went over it, muttering and ticking with a red pencil.

"Okay!" he said at the end. "That looks like a good haul, Officer Bellingham." He went over to the score-sheet pinned on the wall. "Eighteen marks," he said, writing them in.

I breathed a little easier. I had gotten exactly eighteen items, too. At least Brains hadn't licked me in the first test. Then I crossed my fingers as I saw McGurk frowning at the next list—Wanda's.

"You sure these were two different cars, Officer Grieg? *Both* with gift-wrapped packages left in view?"

"Positive! One outside the candy store and the other parked outside the library."

McGurk nodded, satisfied. Wanda sighed with relief. But I still didn't feel relaxed.

If McGurk refused to accept one of *my* items, that would put Brains ahead!

"Okay, Officer Grieg," said McGurk. "I accept all yours. But it only puts you at thirteen."

Brains tittered. "Very unlucky!"

"This isn't the only test!" Wanda flashed back. "There are five more yet—*Little* Brains!"

Then McGurk started on my list. And when he came to the end and wrote "18" after my name, my crossed fingers were so stiff they had pins and needles.

Finally, when McGurk was through with Willie's list, here's how the scoresheet looked:

| NAME OF OFFICER | M A R K S | | | | | |
	Test #1	Test #2	Test #3	Test #4	Test #5	Test #6
BELLINGHAM	18					
GRIEG	13					
ROCKAWAY	18					
SANDOWSKY	11					

Brains's face glowed.

"Looks like only you and me *in* this, Joey!"

"Don't worry, Willie!" said Wanda. "Like I said—there are five more tests yet."

"Yeah!"

"There could be *fifty* more," scoffed Brains. "But *you'd* never catch up, Wanda! No girl could *ever* make Lieutenant in this Organization."

"Oh no?" said Wanda, pulling a second notebook out of her pocket and handing it to Brains. "So how about *this*?"

I saw at once that it was Mari's. Brains riffled through page after page of Japanese writing, his eyes popping.

"There are ten pages of items there, Mr. Bright Boy! Making a total score of thirty-four. Repeat— *thirty-four!*"

McGurk reached out.

"Let *me* see that!" Then he frowned as he flipped through the pages. "Uh—how do we know they're any good?"

"Mari translated them for me," said Wanda. "After getting me to promise not to use any of them if I hadn't already got them myself. And I made notes in English. And here they are."

Then Wanda opened her own book at the back and began to read out.

"Item—ladder left overnight at side of garage of Berg house, inviting use by burglars. Item—brand-new bike left unlocked outside Gallo house. Item— box of expensive tools left open and unguarded on sidewalk underneath where telephone repairmen were at work on pole. Item—man on Main Street with wallet sticking out of back pocket of jeans, inviting pickpockets. . . ."

And so on. Containing some items in our own lists, sure—but so much more that I felt my ears burning. I mean, I'd walked past that repair crew myself. Just down the street from where Brains lives. I'd even seen the toolbox—but without realizing it was a temptation to sneak-thieves. Which it was, of course.

Then I saw that Brains's ears had gone red too, so I didn't feel so bad.

McGurk looked very thoughtful when Wanda came to the end.

"That Mari is one smart kid, I'll say that!"

"Yes, but she isn't a member," said Brains.

"No. . . ." McGurk sounded wistful. "It doesn't count in the official test, of course."

"But it does show that some people *aren't* as good as they think they are!" said Wanda.

This seemed to sting Brains.

"Anyway, *you* should talk!" he said. "One of Mari's examples was in your own house. And that's bad for an officer of a detective organization."

This was true. Mari had scored by pointing out that when a man with the phone company badge on his shirt had come to ask to test the Grieg phones— in connection with the nearby repair work—neither Wanda nor her mother had asked to see his ID card.

"We just didn't think about it," said Wanda.

"That's no excuse, Officer Grieg!" said McGurk. "Uh—did Mari ask to see his ID?"

"She said she would have, if it had been her house. But since she's a guest, it might have looked impolite. Also she figured we must have known him anyway."

"Did you?"

"No. But it was okay. Nothing was stolen."

"Hm! Well, don't forget in the future. It's always best to make sure." He handed over Mari's notebook. "Right, men! Back to the exam. Test Number Two is called—'Skill at Spotting Examples of Suspicious Behavior.'"

6 Suspicious Behavior

"A good detective," McGurk said, "is always quick to spot suspicious behavior. Most times there will be an honest explanation. But a good detective is always curious until he makes sure."

"Do *we* check to make sure?" said Brains. "In the test?"

"No. There won't be time. Like I said, it'll probably be innocent anyway. This is just to see how quick you are to recognize when something looks suspicious."

"Yes," I began, "but—"

But McGurk hadn't finished. Spotting suspicious behavior is *his* strong point. In fact, he is our suspicious behavior expert.

"Lots of people don't even notice when something fishy is going on," he continued. "But *you*—you're detectives. So go to it and check in with your lists same time tomorrow."

"But aren't you overlooking something, McGurk?" I said.

"What?"

"These tests are supposed to be fair. Detective skills only. Not general education."

He frowned.

"Yes. So?"

"So as word expert I can tell you there's no *way* of writing down an account of suspicious behavior in clear, short notes. It takes space. Maybe *pages* just for one example." There was an uneasy stirring around the table. "Now me—I'll be okay. I'm good at writing. But some of us—"

"Yeah!" groaned Willie, who, though he may not be good with words, can put a whole lot of different meanings into just that one. "Yeah!" he said again, with a long sad sigh.

McGurk was nodding.

"All right. So just make a *rough* note of each example. Any old note, so long as it reminds you. Then tomorrow you can *tell* me what you observed. And I'll give you the marks just the same. *If* they deserve any!"

Well, he could have said that again!

I don't know whether *you've* noticed this, but things don't always work out for kids as well as they're supposed to. Like the stuff you read in Things-To-Do books. Where it shows how to do something special and it looks like a breeze.

Until you start trying to do it.

McGurk is always coming up with bright ideas for something to do. And I must admit they often do work. But there are times when McGurk's bright ideas take a regular nose dive, and this was one of them.

Looking back, I can see where he went wrong. I mean the first test had gone pretty well, right?

And why?

Because there are far more honest but careless people around than there are crooks. So there are always lots of examples of careless behavior.

But crooked people are usually cautious. They don't go around advertising what they intend to do. So there aren't nearly so many examples of *suspicious* behavior to be seen. And most of those turn out to be not related to crime, as McGurk himself pointed out.

Anyway, that's just my theory of *why* the test was

a disaster. The actual details of that disaster come next. . . .

The rain didn't help. A fairly heavy shower started about five minutes after we'd left our HQ. This meant we'd had to run to our homes and take cover, and it looked like just so much wasted time.

Even when the shower ended I seemed to be out of luck.

"Joey," said Mom, "we're fresh out of bread. Why don't you bring me a loaf from the supermarket, right away?"

"Aw, Mom—!"

"We *were* going to have tuna sandwiches for lunch, but I suppose you won't mind a salad."

"I'm on my way, Mom!"

"I thought you would be."

But Mom made the wrong deduction there. It wasn't because I just *hate* salads that changed my mind. It was because I remembered that a super-market is probably one of the best places for spotting suspicious behavior.

Sure enough, I'd no sooner picked a loaf off the rack when I saw my first example. It was just across the aisle, where the cookies were stacked. Instead of taking anything *off* the rack, a customer was

putting a couple of packs of chocolate-chip cookies
back.

Well, sometimes customers do change their minds.
But it was the way this lady did it. Swiftly. Furtively.
Then she looked around with a worried frown on
her pale, fat face and I pretended to be reading the
list of ingredients on the loaf wrapper.

I wondered if maybe she was one of those nuts
who go around putting poison in products on supermarket shelves. So, after she'd wheeled her cart
away, I quickly stepped across and put those two
packs to one side, so I could identify them without
delay later.

But first I wanted to get a better look at the suspect. And I was just turning the corner when— back she came, nearly knocking me over.

I pretended to go on my way. But I peered around that corner and saw her going straight back to the same shelf.

She paused. Then suddenly she grabbed two packs of chocolate chips from right next to where she'd replaced the others. Then she tossed them into the cart and moved away again, fast, head down.

"Now that really *is* suspicious!" I decided. "I bet she lost her nerve. I bet she thinks those are the same two she'd doctored, but now she's decided not to go through with it. I bet—"

"*All right, young man! Would you mind telling me what you're doing?*"

I'd nearly flipped when the man's hand dropped on my shoulder.

Then I recognized him as the manager.

"Yes, sir," I said. "That lady who's just gone around there. I've been watching her and—"

"We *know* you've been watching her. And we've been watching *you* on the TV monitor. So what's the explanation?"

When I told him what I'd suspected, he didn't seem impressed.

"That lady is one of our most respected customers," he said. "Mass poisoner! Hah! . . . No.
We're more interested in *your* behavior and you'd
better have a *good* explanation."

Then I realized what a spot I was in. So I told
him everything, showing him my ID card and the
notebook.

Gradually his face brightened up.

"Okay," he said. "I believe you, son. But let me
give you a word of advice. Go play your detective
games someplace else. Not in my store. For your

information, that lady *always* acts like that around the cookies and candies. She's been dieting for years, and she finds them a great temptation. But she always *pays* for them, so why should we worry how many times she takes them off the shelf and puts them back on again?"

"It did look suspicious, though," I said. "You've got to agree to that."

"Oh sure!" Then he laughed. "But not half as suspicious as *your* behavior. You should have seen yourself on the screen!"

Well, that was just about it for the rest of the day for me. In fact the only really suspicious behavior I spotted after that was connected with the other members of the Organization.

Like:

1. Willie Sandowsky, early afternoon, downtown, following an elderly, poorly dressed lady carrying a large black plastic bag. Whenever she stopped, Willie stopped. If I hadn't known him, I'd have sworn Willie was a juvenile purse-snatcher stalking a victim. He even followed her *into* one store, a dry cleaners. But he came out first, blushing.

2. Wanda and Mari, midafternoon, also downtown. They were standing in line at a bus stop. Now I knew the buses that stopped there went in the

opposite direction from where they lived. So I hung around and observed them.

"Are they so strapped for examples they're thinking of trying their luck in another town?" I wondered. "And if so, would it be fair?"

But when the next bus came, they didn't get on it. Or on the next. Or the one after. And the buses at that stop serve one route only. *Very* suspicious!

In the end I realized they were probably using the bus stop as an observation post, where they could keep watch on passers-by without anyone taking much notice of them.

But if I'd been a cop and hadn't known them, I

would have marked them out as a pair of possible international girl pickpockets.

3. Brains Bellingham, late afternoon, sitting on a seat in Willow Park, his head behind a science magazine. Nothing suspicious about that? Normally, no.

But there'd just been another shower and Brains had no coat *and the seat was very wet*. Also the magazine he was pretending to be so interested in was *upside down*!

Obviously, he was keeping observation on someone or something. I looked around to see what might strike him as being suspicious. Then I noticed a movement behind a bush about a hundred yards away and, sure enough, spotted a figure lurking there.

Well, my eyes must be better than Brains's. He

hadn't seen *me* even, so when I said, "Forget it, Brains!" he nearly jumped clear off the seat.

"Uh—whu–what—?"

"It's only McGurk! Checking on us."

McGurk came out of hiding then, looking damp and miserable. I guess even he realized by now what a flop his second test was proving to be.

"How's it going, men?"

"Lousy!" grumbled Brains. "And to think I could be home, getting on with my experiment!"

"I can't say it's a terrific success, McGurk," I said.

"Yeah, well," he grunted. "Stick with it, men, and I might think of giving double marks for this test."

"Big deal!" muttered Brains. "Two times zilch is zilch!"

It made me feel a little better. At least I could claim *one* genuine example.

I wasn't looking forward to the final checking of results, all the same.

Would Mari have whipped us all again?

I suddenly remembered the expression on her face back at the bus stop. Wanda had appeared to me to be under a strain, like the rest of us that afternoon. But Mari had seemed much more composed. Not wreathed in smiles, but very thoughtful, wary, alert—as if even then she was busy registering her sixth or seventh example.

7 Joey's Big Score

Nobody seemed very eager to report the next morning. When I arrived, Wanda was already there—this time with Mari—but there was no sign of Willie or Brains.

It was 9:35. McGurk was in the middle of an argument with Wanda.

"How many times do I have to tell you, Officer Grieg? Mari is *not* a member."

"I know! But you've already agreed she can do the tests for her own amusement."

"Sure, but—"

"And in *this* test we've got to *tell* you our examples. So how can Mari tell you anything if she isn't here?"

"All right, all right!" growled McGurk. "She can stay. Just this one time." He turned to Mari. "Take a seat," he said, gruffly.

Mari's eyes brightened. But she kept silent, simply nodding and sitting down.

I looked at her curiously, wondering how many examples she had spotted.

Then McGurk glared around.

"Anybody seen Brains or Willie? Look at the time, it's—Oh, so you've decided to join us, have you, Officer Sandowsky?"

Willie had just come in. He was looking terribly gloomy. His nose seemed even longer and his head was drooping.

"Yeah!" he mumbled. "Sorry I'm late, McGurk. But I only got one thing yesterday and I was trying to find another this morning."

"Cheer up, Willie!" said Wanda. "I bet Brains doesn't even have *one* example. He'll be calling in sick any minute now. You'll see."

"Anyway," said McGurk, "we can't wait any longer. You're next on the list, Officer Grieg. Tell us what you've got."

"Well, *I* only got one example, too. And let me say right now I think this was a dumb—"

"Just give the example and cut the trimmings, huh?"

Wanda sighed heavily and rolled her eyes.

"Well, this one I found right at the start, before leaving the house. I was looking out of the window, wondering when the shower would be over, and a small panel truck pulled up opposite. Well, not quite opposite. Sort of *diagonally* opposite, I—"

"Yes, yes!" said McGurk. "But the truck—what sort did you say it was?"

"One of those small panel trucks. A Ford—right, Mari?"

Mari nodded.

"A green Ford, yes."

"With no markings," continued Wanda. "Then, after a few minutes, the driver got out, all bundled up against the rain, shut the door, and walked away."

"Where to?"

"Who knows? I watched until he was out of sight. And that was my example."

"Huh!" said Willie. "What's suspicious about that?"

"It was *raining!*" said Wanda. "And there were plenty of parking spaces in the direction he was walking. So why park where he did, instead of nearer to where he was going?"

"How long was it there?" asked McGurk. "I mean had he been delivering it for someone across from you, maybe?"

"No, it wasn't being left there for anyone on our street. In any case, he'd have stopped right outside their house, wouldn't he? And gone to the door to let them know. Anyway, it was gone when we came back from our first outing."

McGurk looked impressed.

"Hm! Pretty good, Officer Grieg. That *was* suspicious. Did you take the license plate number?"

"Yes, just in case—"

"Very good! I'm giving double marks in this test, so that's two for you."

"Mari has the same example," said Wanda, looking pleased. "She noticed the truck too, of course, even without my saying—"

"Sure, sure! But we'll hear her examples when

we're through with the *official* members' reports. . . .
Officer Rockaway, you're next."

I took a deep breath. My big moment was approaching, but I wasn't quite ready.

"That's okay, McGurk," I said. "I have quite a bunch here. You might as well be taking Willie's *one*, while I check over my notes."

They all stared at me, McGurk with hope, Willie and Wanda with surprise and envy, and Mari (who had nothing to lose) with admiration.

"Okay," said McGurk. "But you better not be fooling."

Willie's example turned out to be pretty good.

"Yeah, well," he began, "I was walking along Main Street and this lady passes me. Oldish, sort of poorly dressed, carrying a plastic bag, all bulging. But it was the smell I noticed most. Perfume. Not strong, but sort of lingering. And the suspicious thing was that I *knew* that perfume. One of the most expensive you can buy."

"*How* do you know?" said Wanda.

"Because my Aunt Mabel uses it, and she's very rich, and she once told Mom how expensive that stuff was. I forget its name, but I sure remember the perfume. Nothing else like it."

"Very good, Officer Sandowsky. But are you sure it came from *her*?"

"Absolutely sure!" said Willie. "My nose doesn't make mistakes like that. Anyway, I followed her, just to double check. And, sure enough, it was she. And I was thinking how come a poor old woman like that gets to wear an expensive perfume like this. Was she a rich woman in disguise? Or had she stolen something from a rich woman—something that still had the perfume on it?"

"Did you ever find out?" asked Mari, looking fascinated.

"Yeah!" said Willie. "She was clean. In fact that's where she was going. To the cleaners. I followed her in, just as the clerk was taking these fancy dresses out of the sack. 'So you're still working for Mrs. Van Beuren, Maggie,' he said. 'When's she want them?' So I realized then she was a rich lady's maid."

"Terrific!" McGurk's eyes gleamed. "I'd give you *triple* marks for that, Willie, only it wouldn't be fair to the others."

"That's okay by me," said Wanda. "I thought it was pretty good, too."

"And me!" I said.

So Willie got three marks, and he looked like a dog with three bones.

Then I was ready. Brains still hadn't shown up, and I'd have loved to see his face as he heard my examples. But it seemed Wanda was right. It looked as though our science expert would be calling in sick.

So I told them about the lady in the supermarket. McGurk agreed it was a fair example and gave me two marks.

Then I produced my ace—not to mention my King, Queen and Jack—of trumps.

The ace was when I told them about being collared by the supermarket manager. They all grinned.

"Very funny!" said McGurk. "But let's get on to your second example, Officer Rockaway."

"That's it," I said.

"Huh?"

"Yes. Suspicious behavior, right? *Mine*, admittedly. But suspicious enough for the manager to nearly have me arrested!"

McGurk was frowning, but—

"Yes," he murmured. "Sure. Why not? It *is* a true example."

Even Wanda and Willie had to agree.

Then I produced my King—my next example— and told them of Willie's suspicious behavior.

"I know *now* what he was doing. But it did look very suspicious."

They all had to agree to that, too.

Then I produced my Queen and told them of the suspicious behavior of Wanda and Mari.

Wanda looked a bit miffed, but Mari couldn't restrain herself.

"Ah, so! *Very* good, Joey!"

"Any more, Officer Rockaway?" said McGurk.

"Yes. My Jack—uh—my fifth example."

Then I told them about Brains's antics in the park.

McGurk was looking *very* pleased by now.

"Nice work, Officer Rockaway! Shows real initiative. Five examples—ten marks. Any more?"

I wondered if I dared throw in his own behavior behind the bush. But in all fairness I decided that should belong to Brains. So I shook my head.

"Okay," said McGurk. "Well, while we're waiting for Officer Bellingham—who'd better have a good excuse!—we might as well hear *your* examples, Offic—uh—Mari. Ready?"

She stood up and nodded.

"Only two," she said.

I breathed easier.

"First one you know already," she said. "The truck. The second one—sorry, Wanda—was in bus line. Joey was right. It was good place to observe from. But also someone *else* was observing—"

"Yeah!" said Willie, grinning. "Joey!"

"No," said Mari. "I mean in same line. Because not

only Wanda and I were letting buses go. Also man farther behind. He, too, let buses go. Man with rain hat, floppy all around, and small case."

Wanda was wearing a bashful grin.

"And I was too busy looking all around to notice what was going on a few feet away!" she said.

"Yeah!" McGurk was really tickled. "How about *that*, Officer Rockaway? How come *you* didn't spot this guy while you were watching your fellow officer?"

I felt my face go red. With her one example, Mari had managed to take me down a couple of pegs. But I grinned and nodded to the Japanese girl.

"You beat me there!"

She smiled back.

"I wonder what the guy *was* doing in the line," said Willie.

Wanda shrugged.

"Maybe waiting for someone to *arrive*. But I agree. It does rate as suspicious behavior, and I could have kicked myself when Mari told me about it afterward."

Meanwhile, McGurk had walked over to the scoresheet to enter the marks.

"Brains is going to have to produce some good examples to catch up with me this time," I said.

"Yes," said Wanda. "And it looks like he just might, at that!"

I turned.

Brains was bustling in, waving a sheet of paper.

"Sorry I'm late, McGurk! But just wait till you hear this! Double marks? No way! This deserves quadruple marks! *Oct*uple!"

8 Brains's Bombshell

Something about Brains's manner made us all stare.

Our science expert was flushed. Also sweating. The hand clutching the paper was trembling.

Was he really sick, I wondered. Had he got out of bed in a fever?

I mean, I'd managed to get a peek at that paper, and it was a mess. Like I said earlier, Brains's writing is usually very neat and orderly. But this was like a maze, with lines slanting every which way, and crossings-out, and scribbled additions, and words trailing off into squiggles.

"All right, Officer Bellingham!" said McGurk. "Take it easy. You sure you're feeling okay?"

"Never better!" snapped Brains. "Listen. Let me

tell you what happened. Otherwise you'll never believe me."

"Uh-oh!" murmured Wanda.

"We're listening," said McGurk.

"Well," said Brains, "when I went home from the park yesterday, I was so fed up about the test I decided to get on with my experiment instead."

"What experiment?" said McGurk.

"The one I was telling Mari about—oh, hi, Mari!"

Mari smiled. "The pocket cordless telephone, yes?"

"Yes. Well, it wasn't going so good. In fact it started going all wrong—"

"Aha!" said Wanda.

Brains turned.

"What's *that* supposed to mean?"

"Your oath. May all your experiments go wrong if you cheated on the tests!"

"But I *wasn't* cheating! If I'd been cheating I'd have been sitting down in comfort, *making up* examples—"

"Never mind that, Officer Bellingham! What's on the paper?"

"Listen!" said Brains. "*Please!* . . . I'd been counting on examining the phone in my dad's car. To pick up a few pointers. I have to be careful, because he'd go bananas if he saw me messing around with it.

Well, I took a quick look last night and I thought I saw a way of getting my own idea to work. So this morning, while Mom and Dad were finishing breakfast, I snuck into the garage to check. It meant dialing a local number and I thought of ringing yours, McGurk—"

"So did you?" said McGurk, sharply. "Because *I* never heard—"

"Yes, I did. But no, you wouldn't hear a ring." Brains looked worried. "Because— I don't know. Maybe it was something I did when I opened up the mouthpiece last night. Or maybe it was something to do with all the repair work that's been going on lately. Anyway, I got a crossed line and cut in on someone else's conversation."

"My mother or father?" said McGurk.

"No, no. . . . Complete strangers. Two men. I was trying to say I was sorry, but they couldn't hear. And then—when I realized what they were saying —well. I mean. I thought it was my duty."

"You mean that's a transcript?" I said.

"Yes," said Brains. "As well as I could remember. From when I caught on, to when the fault corrected itself and they went off the line. I've been over it again and again, and I'm sure I've got it word for word now."

Well, the writing was such a mess that McGurk got Brains to read it out. Later he got me to type it, and here is a copy:

```
        PART OF CONVERSATION OVERHEARD BY

        OFFICER GERALD BELLINGHAM

        8:50 A.M., August 2nd.

1st MAN:  So we can make our move at the Senior
          Citizens' Picnic at the Community Hall.

2nd MAN:  You sure she'll be there?

1st MAN:  Sure I'm sure!  There could be a cool
          half million each for us in this.  And I
          don't make mistakes when there's money like
          that on the line.  And hey - you haven't heard
          the best.  What makes it easier yet is this.
          It's going to be a fancy catered affair.

2nd MAN:  So?

1st MAN:  So they'll all sit down together at the same
          time and -
          END OF TRANSCRIPT.
```

"So how about *that* for suspicious behavior?" said Brains.

We had to murmur our agreement.

McGurk slapped the table.

"It's more than a test example! That's evidence of a crime being planned! When's this picnic being held?"

"Friday afternoon," said Wanda. "My mother is one of the organizers. And I was meaning to ask you, McGurk, if you'd suspend the exam that day, because—"

"Forget the exam now, Officer Grieg! This is a *case*!"

I decided then that I'd been wrong earlier, after all. To McGurk, *nothing* is more important than a case. Period. I could tell this just by looking at the gleam in his eyes and the fire in his hair, which seemed to have turned two shades redder.

"Friday, huh? Well, it's obvious what's going to happen, men!"

"What?" said Willie.

"While one of the old lady guests is at the picnic, her home's going to be robbed."

"Nuh-uh!" Brains was shaking his head. "The first man said they'd make their move *at* the picnic. That's definite."

McGurk frowned.

"All right. So this guest is going to be *wearing*

some valuable jewelry. Or carrying valuables in her purse. And they're—"

"A million dollars' worth, McGurk?" said Wanda. "Come on! These aren't wealthy people."

"Maybe the robbers got it wrong," said Willie. "Maybe they're a couple of dummies."

"Even if they do think someone's necklace is worth more than it really is," said McGurk, "even if they *are* dummies, it's a crime just the same. And it's up to us to prevent it."

"By telling the police, I hope!" said Wanda.

"Oh sure!" said McGurk. "But just in case they don't take us seriously or—" He broke off. "Gee!"

he murmured. "I wonder how we could get ourselves invited?"

I grinned. "Not by posing as senior citizens, that's for sure!"

"Excuse me," said Mari, quietly, "but—"

McGurk didn't hear her.

"Couldn't your mother get us in?" he said to Wanda. "As waiters or something? Dishing out the grub?"

"No way!" said Wanda. "There are enough committee ladies for that. I'm the only kid who's been invited to help in that way. And that's only because Mari is booked to do her ventriloquist act there."

"Huh?"

"Yes," said Wanda. "The kids who *will* be going officially are all scheduled to entertain the old folks. Jerry Pierce will be playing his guitar. A bunch of kids from the Priscilla LaRue Dancing Academy will be dancing."

"And Mari, huh?"

"Well, she's so good that Mom asked her specially."

"And," said Mari, a little louder this time, "I have idea. It is this. Chief McGurk and others can come as my assistants. I will use all four dolls. Assistants can pass them to me when required. Also, Joey can help as script adviser. Also, Chief McGurk as technical adviser, because I plan Crime Prevention routine again, this time for old people." She smiled shyly. "I would not do so well without such fine assistants. I will tell Mrs. Grieg this."

Wanda laughed.

"And of course Mom won't think of refusing! For Mari—anything!"

McGurk was beaming.

Then, from the table drawer, he took out the ID card he'd confiscated the other day. He scribbled something on it and handed it to Mari.

Mari's face had gone very still and masklike. But when she read what he'd scribbled, it split open in one big grin of delight.

"Thank you!" she said. "Oh, thank you very much!"

And this is what we read over her shoulder:

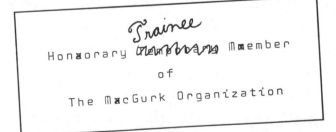

Honorary ~~Temporary~~ *Trainee* Member
of
The MacGurk Organization

"That's all right, Officer Yoshimura," said McGurk. "Now put the card away and pay close attention. We've got work to do."

9 Patrolman Cassidy Studies the Evidence

The first thing we had to do was obvious: tell the police what Brains had overheard.

Brains and some of the others were all for dashing off right away. But McGurk was too much of a cop himself to allow this.

"No, men. The first thing my—uh—our friend Lieutenant Kaspar will want is concrete information. The full details."

"So here they are!" said Brains, waving the paper. "Everything I could remember. Every—"

"No, Officer Bellingham! *Not* everything you could remember. Like for instance, what about the men's voices?"

And so McGurk began to question Brains about whether the voices sounded rough or smooth, old or young, and stuff like that.

This was fair enough, I suppose. But McGurk was so fierce about accuracy, and Brains was still so excited, that they soon clashed.

"You're supposed to be a trained observer, Officer Bellingham! Someone who can come up with hard facts."

"Well, so I did!" howled Brains, waving the paper again. "I got the words accurately, didn't I? I was concentrating on *what* was said, McGurk. Not the *way* they were saying it."

"Look!" said McGurk. "This is only what that lieutenant will ask you. There's no—"

"Excuse me, please!"

Something in Mari's calm voice stopped McGurk short.

"Yes, Officer Yoshimura?"

"As voice expert, may I question?"

McGurk's eyes lit up.

"Hey, yes! You're a *ventriloquist*! Sure! Go ahead!"

Then, once again, Mari showed her value to the Organization.

Still speaking calmly, she began to give samples of various voices. What she said was not always correct English. But every example was terrifically accurate as far as tone, pitch, speed and so on were concerned.

"This is very old voice. . . ." she would begin.

Then:

"Now this is very young voice. . . .

Or:

"This voice very fluent, smooth voice. . . ."

And:

"This voice very—uh—trip-up, stumbling, *hesitant*. . . ."

It was just what Brains needed to help him concentrate. It was also right in his own backyard, something precise, scientific. He became so enthusiastic he asked for a sheet of typing paper and a ruler and, to McGurk's delight, both science expert and voice expert got down to making what Brains called a Voice Profile. With a little help from the word expert, of course.

Here it is—the result of half an hour's careful probing by Mari:

VOICE PROFILE OF SUSPECTS		MAN #1	MAN #2
AGE	YOUNG		
	OLD		
	MEDIUM	X	X
TEXTURE	HARSH	X	
	SMOOTH		X
	MEDIUM		
TONE	DEEP		
	LIGHT		X
	MEDIUM	X	
SPEED	FAST		
	SLOW		X
	MEDIUM	X	
FLOW	FLUENT	X	
	HESITANT		X
	MEDIUM		
PHYSICAL STATE	STRONG	X	
	FEEBLE		
	MEDIUM		X
ACCENT		BOSTON	?.
DEFECTS (LISP, STAMMER etc.)		NONE	? NONE (NOT ENOUGH SPEECH TO BE ABLE TO TELL)

"Now we *can* go to the police!" said McGurk.

When we arrived at the police station we were pleased to see our old friend Patrolman Cassidy in charge of the inquiry desk.

"Hi!" he greeted us. "What is it this time, M'Quirk? Is it a lost child you're bringing in?"

The policeman was looking at Mari. She was looking back with a puzzled frown. I guess she was wondering why, if he was all that big a friend, he'd gotten McGurk's name wrong.

"No, sir. This is Mari Yoshimura. A new trainee member. What we've come about is *this*. . . ."

Then McGurk laid the transcript and the Voice Profile on the desk, and while the cop put on his glasses, McGurk told him how Brains had made the discovery.

"I see," murmured Mr. Cassidy, reading the transcript slowly. "Hm! . . . Yeah. . . . Well. . . ."

With every grunt he was getting to look more doubtful. Finally, he began slowly shaking his head.

"You say this came over on the car phone?" he asked Brains. "Radio phone?"

"Yes, sir."

"Well, you know what I think? You must have cut into some TV or radio drama."

"No, sir," said McGurk. "It mentions the Senior Citizens' Picnic. Which takes place here, in this town, on Friday aft—"

"I know that, M'Turk. Yeah. . . . I see what you mean." Patrolman Cassidy's frown had deepened. "But in that case it wouldn't make any sense at all. No guest would have that kind of money. Not at *our* Senior Citizens' Picnic!"

"That's just what *we* thought," said McGurk. "Until Officer Sandowsky here pointed out an angle that *did* make sense."

Then McGurk told the patrolman about Willie's theory.

Patrolman Cassidy was very sure in his reply.

"No. That doesn't really make sense, either. I've had nearly thirty years' experience with that sort of hood. And I can tell you that dummies like that wouldn't be planning anything so elaborate. If they thought someone had something that valuable they'd go for it when the person was alone. Not with fifty other people around."

Suddenly Mr. Cassidy grinned.

"You know what? I think it just has to be a joke. Couple of guys fooling around."

"But how would they know Brains would be listening in?" I said.

"No. Not a joke on *you* guys. A joke between themselves."

McGurk hesitated. Then:

"Do you think though that if Lieutenant Kaspar took a look at the evidence he might—"

"McGurk," said Mr. Cassidy solemnly (and his use of McGurk's correct name made it sound ominous), "not now. Not this day. Not even this week. We're due for a departmental inspection and the lieutenant is up to his eyebrows in paperwork."

McGurk nodded. He seemed strangely subdued.

"You think—?"

"I think he might go walking up the wall and have *me* thrown out along with you, if I showed him this just now." Mr. Cassidy pushed the papers back. "No. Forget it. It's obviously a joke. Doesn't make sense, otherwise."

Brains sighed.

"They didn't sound like they were fooling to *me*."

"Anyway," said the policeman, "I'll be patrolling that area Friday afternoon and I'll look in on the picnic. And if you hear any strangers around with voices like this," he tapped the Profile, "just let me know, huh?"

"Well, that's what I call a brush-off!" said Brains, out on the street.

"Don't worry, Officer Bellingham," said McGurk. "All it means is that we'll have to tackle this case on our own."

He even looked pleased. His eyes were gleaming.

"Well, we did our duty," said Wanda. "And I must say Mr. Cassidy made sense over the dummy theory. So what does that leave us with, McGurk?"

"Just a couple of guys joking," murmured Willie. He sighed. "Yeah. I guess that's all it can be."

"Wrong, Officer Sandowsky!" The gleam brightened. "That is *not* all!"

"What then?" I said.

"This," said McGurk. "It came to me in there. Maybe the guys *do* know what they're doing."

"How?"

"Like maybe one of the guests does have some very valuable stuff but doesn't realize it. Like maybe a family heirloom. Maybe she took it to get it appraised. Maybe one of the guys was the expert she went to. And maybe he decided to keep quiet about its real value. So he could steal it later."

McGurk looked around at us with an unbelievably crafty smile.

"Yeah!" growled Willie.

"Ah!" murmured our new member, gazing at McGurk with admiration.

"Makes sense," I said.

Wanda raised the only objection.

"But in that case the man wouldn't *need* to steal it. All he'd have to do was say it was worth a few hundred dollars and offer to *buy* it. A poor person would jump at the chance."

"Not if it were a family heirloom," I said. "With sentimental value."

"Then again," said McGurk, with an even craftier grin, "maybe this guest could be someone who's only *acting* poor. Maybe an old girlfriend of one of the big-time gangsters. Someone with a whole bunch of valuable loot left over from the old days. But keeping quiet about it, naturally."

Now there were more than Mari gazing at him with admiration.

"Wow!" said Wanda. "Do you think we'd better go back in there and—"

"And get the brush-off again?" said McGurk. "No way! At least not until we have concrete information that the police *can't* laugh off." He frowned. "Officer Grieg, your mother is on the picnic committee. Do you think you could get hold of a copy of the guest list?"

10 McGurk Gets Ready

Right after lunch, Wanda brought a guest list over and we went through it, name by name.

"Remember, men," said McGurk, "we need to pinpoint two different types. One: old ladies with heirlooms that could be worth more than they think. And two: old ladies who might have run around with gangsters when they were young."

Well, the first task was hopeless. I mean, nearly everyone owns some old family ornaments and stuff.

In the end, McGurk shook his head.

"We'll skip that category for now. Let's move on to possible ex-criminal types."

This was difficult too. It was almost impossible to imagine most of those old ladies being gun molls

in their younger days. But after a while McGurk was
able to circle two names. These:

```
Mrs. Bronson
Mr. & Mrs. Brunning
(Mrs. Cape)
Mr. & Mrs. Cevill
```

```
Mr. Martin
Miss Phillips
(Ms. Quinn)
Mrs. Radowicz
```

One reason was that both ladies liked to wear a
lot of junk jewelry. Most of us wouldn't have known
it was junk, but Wanda was very positive.

"It's just cheap stuff," said Wanda. "Anyone can
see that. I mean you can buy things just like it in the
pharmacy. For a few dollars."

McGurk nodded.

"Maybe. Maybe not. Maybe most of their stuff *is*
cheap. But what better hiding place for some real
jewelry than among a whole lot of junk jewelry?"

Another reason for pinpointing those two ladies
was their manner. Mrs. Cape lived alone and liked
to keep to herself. Nobody knew where she'd come
from, or who or what Mr. Cape had been when
he was alive. She didn't have any special friends
and, as far as any of us knew, she'd never been
visited by relatives.

"It's a wonder she ever agreed to go to the picnic
at all," said Wanda.

"Possibly just shy?" suggested Mari.

"Possibly!" grunted McGurk. "But come Friday afternoon we keep a close watch on her."

As for Ms. Quinn—Ms. Sadie Quinn—her manner was just the opposite. There was nothing secretive or shy about *her*. She was a big, fairly fat lady, who dyed her hair a dazzling yellow and always wore lots of make-up. And the only reason you could be sure she was a senior citizen under all that disguise was because she was always bragging about it.

"Who'd believe I was seventy-four, huh?"

Or:

"I could give you a fifty-yard start, young man, and still lick you in a two-hundred-yard dash!"

She's said stuff like that to me, and she's said it

to other kids. She never *does* kick off her high-heel shoes and race with anyone, though. In fact, she once got mad when Willie took her seriously and said, "All right, Ms. Quinn—come on, then!"

Then she gave Willie a real mouthful, asking him who he thought he was, talking to his elders like that, so that poor Willie did that dash anyway, just to get out of range.

"Yeah!" he said now. "She *could* have been a gangster's girlfriend, I bet! My mom says she told her she used to be a belly dancer in a nightclub."

McGurk nodded.

"We keep an eye on *her!*" he said.

After that, McGurk decided it was time to study the layout of the Community Hall.

"The scene of the crime-to-be," he called it. "And keep your eyes open for anyone *else* who seems to be studying the layout!" he added darkly.

Well, there were no sinister strangers hanging around when we got there. There was nobody around at all except for Mr. Healey, the janitor, who was cutting the grass on the front lawn.

But it gave us a good excuse for prowling around when he said, "Hi, Wanda! Looking for your mom? I think she left earlier, but you can take a look inside if you like. The door's open."

"Is this where the picnic's going to be, sir?" asked McGurk. "On the front lawn?"

"Yeah," said the man. "If the weather holds up. My guess is we'll be having it in the hall."

It was quite a simple layout and it didn't take me long to make a rough sketch. Later, I drew it more carefully for our records. It turned out to be very important in connection with what happened on Friday afternoon. Here's a copy:

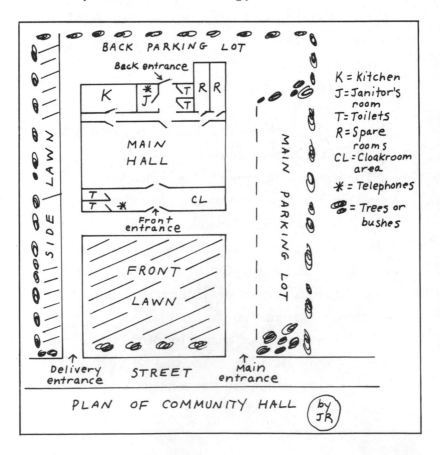

PLAN OF COMMUNITY HALL (by JR)

McGurk was very concerned about the exact location of the phones. The one in the janitor's room was for official business. The one in the front lobby was a pay phone.

"You sure there aren't any more?" he asked Wanda.

"Positive," she replied. "What's so special about them, anyway?"

We were standing in the empty main hall. All the tables and chairs were folded and stacked along one of the side walls. It seemed very quiet and peaceful.

"When the action starts on Friday," said McGurk, "there'll be no time to go looking around for phones. Every split second could count!"

We listened in silence. McGurk seemed so very certain that something *would* happen, it sort of got to us.

Suddenly the place didn't seem all that peaceful anymore.

As we left the building, it started to sprinkle. So we ran back to our HQ and began the next phase of McGurk's preparations.

"There's only one full day between now and Friday, men," he said. "So I guess it's time we started rehearsing the talking dolls act."

"We, McGurk?" said Wanda.

"You bet!" said McGurk. He turned to Mari. "Didn't you say something about needing my advice as crime expert, Officer Yoshimura?"

"Yes, Chief McGurk!" Mari's eyes were shining. "Crime against old people. I wondered if—"

"Right!" said McGurk. "Well, one of those crimes is exactly what we were talking about before. Phony experts offering to buy old family trinkets. Only being prepared to cheat or steal. Taking advantage of old people. Think you could handle that?"

"Sure!" said Mari. "One doll as old lady victim. Another as crook, knocking on door." She wiggled her left hand like she had a doll on it. "Knock! knock!" (Just like knuckles on wood!) "Yes, what do you want, young man?" (All thin and quavery, like a feeble old woman!) "Lady, I pay very good prices, many dollars, for old jewelry and—"

"Terrific!" said McGurk. "We'll work out the exact details later. But what *we* do—the rest of us—is watch that audience like hawks when Mari is doing this routine. Because if any of those ladies *have* been approached by this kind of crook lately, this will remind them. And they'll show it!"

Here, McGurk went into one of *his* acts.

"They'll gasp!" he gasped. "They'll turn pale!

They'll grab hold of their necklaces or bracelets or whatever, realizing what a narrow escape they've had! Especially if Mari makes the crook doll *really* nasty."

Mari giggled.

"I can do that, Chief McGurk!" She made her left hand bend to one side, and out from between the second and third fingers came a voice so creepy I felt myself shiver: *"Yeh! heh! Watch me cheat this foolish old lady who thinks I am nice young man! And when I have cheated—maybe I cut her throat to keep her quiet! Yeh! heh! heh!"*

Even McGurk looked a bit taken aback.

"Yeah! Good! Uh—what was I saying?"

"Watching the audience, McGurk," whispered Brains, staring at Mari's hand.

"Oh—yes! Well, that's how we'll be able to pin-point any possible targets of *that* kind. Watching the audience reaction. Keeping our eyes open!"

It seemed to me that our eyes were going to be working overtime, what with watching Mrs. Cape and Ms. Quinn so closely, and now the rest of the old ladies.

But it sounded like a fairly good idea, so we all set to work eagerly, helping Mari get her act together.

11 Ideal Conditions for a Crime

Now, here is a weather report. One that made an important difference.

All day Thursday it rained. There was a foggy sort of break on Thursday night, but on Friday morning it was raining steadily again.

So we were not surprised when Wanda and Mari showed up at ten o'clock with the news that the picnic was being switched to inside the hall.

"Even if the rain stops in the next half-hour," said Wanda, "it'll be too late. The lawn will be too soggy."

What *did* surprise us, though, was the scene that awaited us—McGurk, Willie, Brains and myself—

when we arrived at the hall at 3:15 that afternoon.

The committee had set up our arrival time.

"The doors will be opened for guests at 3:30," Wanda had explained. "My mom and the other committee ladies will be there much earlier, to start preparing the meal. As one of the helpers, so will I, together with Mari. But the rest of you won't be admitted until 3:15, along with the other kid performers. My mom doesn't want them hanging around too long before their acts."

"When will that be?" asked McGurk.

"In two stages—"

"Take all this down," McGurk said to me. "The timetable could be important."

So I did, and it was, and here it is:

SENIOR CITIZENS' ANNUAL
PICNIC (RAIN PROGRAM)
3:15 Doors open to entertainers.

3:30 Doors open to guests.

4:00 – 4:30 Entertainment (Pt. 1)

4:30 – 5:15 Meal

5:15 – 6:15 Entertainment (Pt. 2)

Anyway, we got quite a shock when we arrived—right on time, all spruced up—to see so many cars already in the parking lot, with others arriving even as we gaped.

"Hey!" said McGurk. "What *is* this?"

"Maybe there's been another change of plan," said Brains. "With the sun coming out before lunch, they might have decided to hold the picnic outdoors after all."

"It doesn't look like it to me," I said, pointing to the empty lawn, glistening wetly in the sun.

"Wait till I get hold of Officer Grieg!" growled McGurk. "Misinforming us like this!"

Wanda was waiting just inside the door to the main hall, looking very worried. She was holding a tray loaded with empty soft drink cans. Behind her, more than a couple of dozen old folks were either sitting around at tables or drifting about.

"All right, Officer Grieg! What's the story?"

"I'm sorry, McGurk! It wasn't my fault. I gave you the right details. But some of the guests got it wrong. Maybe with the weather brightening up. They started arriving soon after two-thirty and we couldn't just turn them away."

"How about my Seven Up, young lady?" Gramp Martin, the local grouch, barked from a nearby table.

"Coming soon, Mr. Martin!" said Wanda, moving toward the back.

We followed her.

"Some even expected to be having the picnic out on the lawn after all," Wanda continued. "I mean, just look at them!"

Quite a few ladies were dressed in shorts and halter tops. Most of the men were in bright sport shirts.

McGurk was still annoyed.

"You could have called us!" he said.

Wanda nearly dropped the tray, she flung back her hair so angrily.

"Hah! *When?* I've been run off my feet ever since we got here. The kitchen's in chaos. The microwave oven's on the blink. Some of the early arrivals have been getting restless. It's been go-go-go every second!"

"Where's Mari?" I asked.

"And that's another thing," said Wanda. "Most of the performers. *They* got here too early, too. And now some of *them* are getting uptight."

"Why?" said Willie.

"Because of the delay. The committee has had to rearrange the program yet again. The meal's being moved up to four o'clock and the entertainment won't start now until that's out of the way. It's

murder back there! Mom's fit to be tied! So be warned!"

McGurk was nodding grimly.

"Yeah!" he muttered, glancing around. "Ideal conditions for a heist. Lots of confusion. And remember, men. *They* know the target. *We* don't. All *we* can do is keep our eyes peeled. Let's start circulating."

"But—" Wanda began, looking alarmed.

But a lady tapped her on the shoulder and demanded to know where her sugar-free cola was. And by the time Wanda had turned back we were already moving around.

Nobody took much notice of us at first. Other helpers were too busy—bringing drinks, moving chairs, taking shawls, bringing them back, opening windows, closing them. Because, believe me, some of our local senior citizens are pretty lively when it comes to keeping their juniors on the hop!

"Pay special attention to Mrs. Cape and Ms. Quinn," said McGurk. "But take note of any others wearing what looks like expensive jewelry. . . . Has Mrs. Cape arrived yet, by the way?"

"Yes. Over in the corner there," said Brains.

Mrs. Cape was sitting alone—hunched up, suspicious, clutching a large, bulging handbag.

"That's where her *real* valuables will be," said McGurk. "If she's brought any. Out of sight."

"Ms. Quinn certainly isn't keeping *her* stuff out of sight!" I said.

She was standing near us. She wore a bright green mini dress and a big orange silk scarf around her hair, with shoes to match. She had the usual collection of rings, chains and necklaces. Plus a huge bracelet that looked like it was studded with emeralds.

She was showing this to two ladies sitting at a table.

"An Egyptian royal prince gave me this," she said. "While I was touring his country with the Bluebell Girls. The jerk said it was real emeralds but I'd heard *that* story before. Anyway, it's the thought that matters." She gave a great gusty sigh. "And the memories! . . . He put it on my wrist one moonlit night in the shadow of the Pyramids."

"Bluebell Girls?" said one of the ladies.

"Yeah. Dancers," said Ms. Quinn. "Hey—and talking of dancers—when do we get the entertainment? Huh?" She unzipped her shoulder bag. "Why don't we liven the joint up?" she said, pulling out a small cassette player. "Some *real* music!"

She switched it on. The opening blare made a lot of people turn. It was one of those old swing-era things. "In the Mood," I think it's called.

Some people groaned. Some rather faded eyes lit up.

Willie was one of those who groaned.

"Huh! Music? That old stuff came *out* of the Pyramids!"

He didn't say it loud, but Ms. Quinn spun around.

"I heard that, young Willie!" she yelled, grinning savagely. "C'm here!"

Then she grabbed his right arm at the wrist, dragged him to the space in the middle of the floor and started dancing with him.

Dancing?

Jitterbugging is what it's called.

Beating up on him is what it looked like.

Poor Willie!

She pulled him, pushed him, spun him around, swung him down on the floor, hauled him up again and generally gave him a thorough working over. I could hear him gasping as he whirled past us. Once, when she'd left him in a heap to do some twirling

of her own, McGurk said, "Try and get a closer look at that bracelet, Officer Sandowsky."

I don't think Willie even heard him. Anyway, the next moment Ms. Quinn was threshing him around once more. So it was a bit like asking someone caught up in the works of a harvesting machine to see if one of the wheels needed oiling.

Some of the crowd loved it. There were hoarse cheers.

Some didn't. There were complaints.

There must have been.

Because the next thing we knew, Mrs. Grieg was marching up to us.

"What do you think you're doing!" she snapped, zeroing in on McGurk. "Can't you see we've enough to cope with without you and your friends getting underfoot? I've a good mind to ask you to leave! Right now!"

12 The Masked Men

Mrs. Grieg is tall and thin. She wears glasses with neat gold rims that make her look calm and cool. Usually she is, too. But not on *that* afternoon.

That afternoon, she was all steamed up.

"I thought you'd come to help Mari!" she said. "So why don't you join her? Now!"

McGurk hated to leave the room where he felt sure a crime would take place. But the thought of being thrown off the premises altogether was even worse.

"Yes, ma'am. Sorry! Come on, men!"

"I warned you!" said Wanda, coming in with another load of drinks just as we were leaving. She jerked her head toward the spare rooms. "Mari's in the one on the left."

Then, as we were crossing the corridor, Mr. Cassidy came out from the kitchen. He was carrying a paper cup.

"Hi, McCork!" he said. "How's it going? Has the stick-up started yet? Ha! ha!"

McGurk looked bitter. For once, he glared at Mr. Cassidy with the disapproval he often aims at us. But before he could say anything, another old tune started to blare from Ms. Quinn's cassette player.

"Ah!" said Mr. Cassidy. "They're playing my song!"

Then he drained the cup, stuck it over his top lip, making it look like a big nose, and went into the main room.

There were hoots and screams of laughter.

The party seemed to be going with a swing for everyone but us.

"Very funny!" grunted McGurk. "Let's hope he's still around when the *real* trouble starts!"

But as soon as we got inside the back room, we could see that some of the performers weren't exactly having a ball either.

Over in a far corner, a group of girls in hula skirts were trying to console a little one who was sobbing and saying she wanted out.

At the other far corner, some bigger girls in ballet skirts were practicing steps to music coming from *their* cassette player.

Nearer the door, Jerry Pierce was strumming chords on his guitar. He had his head cocked to one side and his face seemed twisted with agony. Even as we entered, he turned and yelled at the older girls:

"Turn that thing *down*, will ya? How can a guy get properly tuned up?"

And in the middle of all this, cool and serene, Mari was standing at the side of a small table, silently practicing moves with a couple of dolls.

She was wearing the outfit with Japanese writing on the T-shirt and headband.

"Everything okay, Officer Yoshimura?" asked McGurk, glancing over his shoulder, obviously itching to be back where he thought the action would be.

"Fine, Chief McGurk!" said Mari, smiling. Then she frowned. "But should you not be keeping watch in big room?"

"Huh!" grunted McGurk. "Tell *Mrs. Grieg* that! She—"

He was interrupted by one of the bigger girls. I hadn't recognized her at first, with her hair done up like a ballet dancer's, but it was our old enemy, Sandra Ennis.

"Why, what are *you* doing here, McGurk?" she said, coming across on her toes and twirling around. "Going to give us a clowns' act?"

"We're here on official Organization business," I said.

"*What* official business?" sneered Sandra. She did another tippy-toe twirl. "Bodyguards to Wanda's little friend?"

McGurk blinked. I was sure he'd blow up then. But no. He seemed to check himself. His frown suddenly deepened.

"Ignore her, men!" he murmured.

Sandra ignored *him*. She turned to Mari and, smiling sweetly, said:

"You're Japanese, aren't you? What does that thing say on your shirt?"

Mari smiled back, then at me.

"Joey asked me that. Now I can tell. It say, *McGurk Organization*."

"Huh?"

McGurk stared.

"Yes," said Mari. "I had it specially printed in Tokyo. Before coming."

"A likely story!" Sandra jeered. Her smile wasn't so sweet now. It had once been *her* ambition to join the Organization. "She's conning you, McGurk. Who'd go to *that* expense?"

"What is *conning*, please?" Mari asked me, quietly.

"Cheating," I said. "Tricking. Lying. But don't pay any—"

"I *not* conning!" said Mari, so loud that it made the little girl in the corner jump and start sobbing again.

"Mari's father could buy her a whole T-shirt *factory*!" said Brains. "So why shouldn't she have a special one made?"

"And *she's* a member?" said Sandra. "Well, well! You *must* be having hard times, McGurk!"

Then Mari wiped the smirk right off Sandra's face.

"That girl," said the little old lady doll on her right hand, "is very, very *rude!*"

"You would like for me to kick her?" said the crook doll on her left, in his nastiest voice. "Stomp on her toes?" he added, advancing jerkily toward Sandra.

Sandra backed off, flatfooted. She gaped at the dolls. Then stared at Mari. Then, making a big effort, she shrugged her shoulders—and hurried off back to her corner.

"Well," I said, "I suppose we'd better just stay in here and wait until Mari goes in to do her act."

"Uh—what?" McGurk looked a bit glassy-eyed. "Sorry. I was just thinking of something. A whole new angle. But I need time to—"

Here we had another interruption.

Wanda had come in, looking flushed.

"Mom's sent me! Another crisis! They haven't put enough chairs out! She wants you boys to make yourselves useful and bring another bunch out of the janitor's room."

McGurk's eyes lit up.

"Sure! It'll be a pleasure. But take it easy, men. The longer we can make it last, the more time we'll be able to spend in there."

Well, it was like the senior citizens were in league with us. They were so picky about where they'd like the extra chairs—changing their minds every half-minute—that it looked like it would go on for hours.

In fact, we were still busy when the balloon men arrived.

McGurk was next to me, and the way he gripped my arm nearly made me holler.

"Hey!" he said. "This could be *it*!"

The two men were just entering, with the strings

to dozens of balloons in each hand. The balloons floated above them in a colored cloud.

But it wasn't the balloons we were staring at. It was the masks the men wore.

Rubber carnival masks. One of Mickey Mouse, the other of Groucho Marx.

"That's one of the most common disguises used!" said McGurk.

"By crooks, right?" said Willie.

"Yeah! *Especially stick-up men!*"

13 The Wrong Scent

Most of the other people seemed pleased about the balloon men. There were cries of delight. Even Mrs. Grieg was smiling.

"What a lovely surprise!" she said.

"A gift from the Lions Club, ma'am," said "Mickey Mouse."

"Are they for us?" said Ms. Quinn.

"Sure are!" said "Groucho Marx." "Here, lady! Take one."

As Ms. Quinn reached out, her bracelet shimmering, McGurk said:

"Watch her! And him! I'm going to warn Mr. Cassidy!"

Mr. Cassidy had been talking to Gramp Martin. When McGurk whispered something in his ear, the cop straightened up and let out a bellow of laughter.

"Hey, Charley!" he yelled across to "Mickey Mouse." "These kids think you're a holdup man!"

"Really?" said the man, pulling off his mask.

Then everyone started laughing.

It was Captain Thomas of the Salvation Army, himself an ex-policeman.

"I'm not sure myself about Groucho here," he said, grinning.

The cloud of balloons bobbed as the second man pulled off his mask.

"Phew! That's better!" he said.

We recognized him then, too.

It was Mark Westover, a local newspaper reporter.

"*You've* been watching too much TV, son!" said Captain Thomas.

McGurk's face was red.

"Well, you can't be too careful!" he muttered.

Mr. Westover had turned to Mrs. Grieg.

"We timed it so I could get pictures of the children dancing for the guests."

"Oh dear!" said Mrs. Grieg. "We've had to re-arrange the schedule. The entertainment won't be until after five now."

"That's okay," said the reporter. "I'll look in again."

"Better make it well *after* five," said Mrs. Grieg, gloomy again. "Closer to five-thirty."

Then she turned to the rear door, where Wanda was trying to shoo back a bunch of curious performers.

"That's all right, Wanda," she said. "Come on, you fairies! You can help give out the balloons."

The kids came forward in a rush.

"But we aren't *fairies*, Mrs. Grieg," said Sandra Ennis, on her toes again. "We're cygnets. Young swans."

"Whatever!" said Mrs. Grieg. "So long as you make it snappy!" She turned to the visitors. "Why don't you come back to the kitchen? You look like you could use a cold drink."

When they'd gone, we went back to distributing the extra chairs. This was even slower now, because a lot of the guests were tying their balloons to the backs of chairs already there. Also, the dancers were getting in the way.

Even Mari had come to help, with an arm around the little sobbing girl, who'd looked much happier at first. But very soon she was sobbing again, after Ms. Quinn had popped a balloon right behind her.

"Come on! Hurry it up!" said Mrs. Grieg, returning. "We're almost ready to serve—" Then she broke off, looking toward the rear door. "Oh no! Not *another* bunch of surprise gifts!"

Two men stood there, grinning. They wore lilac-colored coveralls with the words FONAFLOWER INC. on the breast pockets, and they each carried a huge flat cardboard tray piled high with red roses.

Mrs. Grieg had managed to smile again.

"How lovely!" she said. "For us?"

"Yes, ma'am," said the taller, dark-haired man. "Senior Citizens' Picnic, right? A gift from a well-wisher. Prime red roses. Bouquets for the ladies, buttonholes for the men. Right, Mac?"

The other man nodded. He was shorter, tubby, with a sandy mustache.

The dark man looked around.

"Sorry we're late," he said. "We tried to get here for the start of the meal at four o'clock, but—"

"That's all right, sighed Mrs. Grieg. "Nothing's on time today."

"What's wrong?" I asked McGurk. He'd gripped my arm again and was staring at the dark man. "Think *he's* disguised?"

McGurk shook his head.

"No, but—" Then he asked the same question. "What's wrong, Willie?"

Willie was staring at the flowers.

"Strong perfume," he muttered. "*Very* strong!"

"All right, you boys," said Mrs. Grieg. "Help these gentlemen give out the roses. You others, too."

So there came another burst of confusion. Some kids started giving the bouquets to the men and the single ones to the women. The sobbing girl pricked her finger and howled. Then first one senior citizen, then another, started sneezing.

"Take it easy, Mrs. Korbel!" said Mr. Cassidy, going to the aid of one of them. "I guess you must be allergic."

"Bud I—bud I—ASHOO!" went Mrs. Korbel.

And:

"ASHOO!"

and:

"KRISHOO!"

came from other parts of the room.

"Hey!" growled Willie, glaring down at one of the bunches. "*McGurk!*"

"What?"

But before Willie could reply another disaster struck.

There was the sound of a crash. The short man seemed to have tripped and his tray had dropped out of his hands, sending roses scattering all over the floor.

"Give him a hand, you kids!" said the dark man. "They're getting tromped on."

"I'll go get some more from the truck," said his companion.

"Yeah! Do that, Mac. Bring a tray of the pink ones. Maybe they won't cause so much sneezing."

McGurk was kneeling down, pretending to pick up some of the roses.

"Keep your eyes on Ms. Quinn, Joey," he said. "I'll cover Mrs. Cape. This is just the time when a snatch could be made."

"Do you suspect *these* guys?"

"I don't know." McGurk looked harassed. "I mean —well—yeah! Why not? How come *they* knew the new schedule?"

"You mean—?"

"But they seem more bothered about the roses than anyone's jewelry, McGurk," said Wanda.

"Yeah!" growled Willie, still staring at the bunch in his hand. "And so am I!"

McGurk's eyes lit up.

"Yes? Why, Officer Sandowsky?"

"Well. . . ." Willie sniffed. "They don't smell right. This sort shouldn't have any perfume."

"So they've been sprayed with artificial perfume," said Wanda. "So what? They do it all the time at florists."

"Sure! But these guys must have used the wrong spray. This is *carnation* perfume. Which is dumb."

"Yeah! Dumb if you're a *real* florist!" muttered McGurk, staring at the dark man's back. "I think—"

"Hey!" Willie had picked up another bunch. His

nose was wrinkled. "And this one, it smells—*ashoo!* —of *snuff!*" He tossed it down. "*It's been doctored!*"

McGurk looked grim as he peered through the legs of the dancing kids and the others milling around.

"Where's the other guy?"

"Gone to get a fresh supply from the truck," said Wanda.

"I know that. But he's taking his time."

"Yes," said Brains. "But I suppose he's having to

sort out the pink roses. He asked someone to give him a hand. I said I would but he'd already picked Mari."

"*What?*"

McGurk had frozen, still on his hands and knees. When he spoke again it was in a low hoarse rasp.

"But—but that's *it*! That's the caper! It isn't jewels they're after. I can see it as clear as anything now. It's *Mari!*"

14 McGurk Works It All Out

Well, McGurk was sure of himself this time.

"Suddenly everything clicked together," he said, when it was all over. "All the things that had been at the back of my mind. Making me uneasy.

"Like Number One: the 'she' the men were talking about on the phone. Just because it was a Senior Citizens' Picnic, we thought it had to be a guest. Even when our common sense told us that no guest at *that* picnic had *that* kind of money."

"Even the committee helpers weren't in the million-dollar jewelry category, either," I said.

"No," said McGurk. "The only 'she' in that category was Mari. Mari, whose father is head of a worldwide multimillion-dollar business. *She* was the valuable property that was going to be snatched. . . . Anyway," his face became thoughtful, "none of this hit me until near the end."

"When Mari disappeared, right?" said Willie.

"Not quite," said McGurk. "Something started stirring a few minutes earlier. Remember? When Sandra Ennis made that crack about our being bodyguards? And then Brains said something about Mr. Yoshimura being very wealthy?"

McGurk looked wistful.

"But it only stirred. It didn't click. If it had clicked *then* we would have been able to alert the cops right away. Save all the terrible trouble that did happen." He groaned. "But it didn't click until the very last second!"

"You—you can't blame yourself, McGurk," said Wanda, sympathetic for once.

"Anyway," said McGurk, "*when* it clicked—in that one sudden flash—everything became clear. All the other stuff that had been bugging me. Because once I realized it was a big kidnaping caper, it also figured that this would be a very high-powered, well-planned crime."

"Like—"

"Like the trouble and expense they went to to

check on all Mari's movements," said McGurk. "How do you think they found out about her going to the picnic? And all the details of the picnic itself, including the last-minute changes?"

"They bugged the Grieg house, that's how!" said Brains, looking mad with himself. "And I didn't even think of it!"

"Right!" said McGurk. "And that accounts for the phony repairman that Mari spotted. Because he *was* a phony! . . . Anyway," he continued, "that's how they knew all about the plans for the picnic. The van that parked opposite the Grieg house was being used as a mobile listening-in post, once the bugs were planted."

"It figures!" groaned Brains.

But McGurk was addressing Wanda.

"When you saw the driver leave it, you assumed it was empty, right? . . . But if you'd been able to see inside the back you'd have had a shock."

"But the van was only there that one time," said Wanda.

"Sure! But maybe the guy inside heard you and Mari snooping around it, and he decided to try another location. That would have been possible, wouldn't it, Officer Bellingham?"

"Yes," said Brains. "The signal wouldn't have been

as strong, but they could have parked the van on any of the nearby streets and still listened in."

"Another thing," said McGurk, grimly. "Being professionals, they weren't losing any chances of making things easier. Kidnapers usually make the snatch when the victim is out alone somewhere. And if it had been in her own hometown, they'd probably have had plenty of chances of getting Mari that way. But not here. Not as a young visitor in a strange country. Kids her age don't usually go out alone in those circumstances."

"Oh, boy!" murmured Wanda. "So—"

"So everywhere Mari went, you were with her. Naturally. Even between our HQ and your house, that very first morning. . . . But for the first few days at least, they decided to put a tail on you. Just on the off-chance that you'd get separated. Remember the guy in the bus line?"

Wanda and I hung our heads. If only we'd paid more attention *then*!

"But don't worry," said McGurk. "Even Mari, who did notice him, never suspected that *she* was the target."

"What I'm not quite sure about, though," said Wanda, "is why they chose the picnic, with all those people around."

"Exactly *because* there were all those people around," said McGurk. "If they'd snatched Mari when she was out with you, the alarm would have been raised immediately. But with dozens of people, all hassling around—plus lots of confusion, which they certainly knew how to create—well. . . . The chances were that Mari wouldn't be missed for ten minutes or more. Plenty of time for a smooth getaway."

As I said, this discussion took place later, after the hoo-hah was all over. So it was very easy for him to sound so sure of the details. But what McGurk said next was very true.

"Remember, though, all this came in a flash at a very awkward time. I mean—well. . . . You want to know the difference between solving a mystery *after* a crime has been committed and solving a mystery *before* it has been committed?"

"I guess—uh—" Brains began.

"I'll tell you," said McGurk. "In mysteries *after* the crime there's usually plenty of time. The damage has already been done. But with mysteries *before* the crime has even been committed, there's very little time to work in. Once you've seen the solution, the danger could be only minutes away. Like that Friday."

He was right. In fact the danger was only *seconds* away.

So there was no time for McGurk to go into explanations then, as he sprang up off his knees from among the scattered roses. And no time for questions. The look on his face was enough to have us all springing up with him as he said:

"Come on! We've got to find Mari before it's too late! She might even get *killed!*"

15 Mari Springs a Surprise

We headed for the rear. And because one of the men was still in the room, pretending to fuss over the fallen flowers, McGurk had the presence of mind to put on the brakes.

"*Easy*, Willie!" he said, grabbing that boy by the sleeve. "Try not to alert the guy in here."

So we walked as if we had lead weights in our shoes, slow but straining forward. And if it hadn't been for the general confusion, I guess that would have looked strange in itself, alerting the dark-haired man.

But his back was still toward us as we made it into the corridor. *Then* we moved.

"Back parking lot, men!" said McGurk.

And we flew after him like missiles from a sling-shot.

Then, as soon as we got outside, McGurk suddenly put on the brakes again, spreading out his arms.

"Approach with caution, men!"

There were a few cars back there, but only one van, fairly small, plain, dark red.

The back door was closed. There was no sign of anyone in the cab.

"Maybe they had a backup car," I said. "Maybe the other guy's already taken her away."

McGurk shook his head.

"I doubt it. *That's* where he'd lure her first. Into the back of the van."

As he said this, McGurk was advancing on tip-toe. We did likewise. Anyone seeing us then might have thought we were aping Sandra Ennis and her bunch of cygnets.

When we reached the van, McGurk put his ear to the side. I did the same.

Then McGurk gripped my arm again. It was black and blue for days afterward, but I didn't even feel any pain at the time.

"Hear that?" he whispered.

I nodded.

There had been the sound of stealthy movements, followed by the low rasp of a man's voice.

This was followed by another voice—clearer, younger.

"You make big mistake—"

"Shut up!" came the man's voice.

"Mari!" whispered Wanda. "She's—she's in there all right!"

McGurk looked around. Now his expression was very anxious, almost scared.

"Willie—go bring Mr. Cassidy! Quick! Brains—see if they left the keys in the ignition. If they did, get them! Joey—"

Just then there came a bellow from the back door of the building.

"HEY! WHAT D'YOU THINK YOU'RE DO-ING?"

Willie was still halfway there. The dark-haired man made as if to block Willie's path. But Willie was too quick. He may think and talk slow some-times, but he's very fast on his feet, and he neatly dodged the outstretched arm.

The man must have decided not to waste any time on him. He was coming forward rapidly now, his face hard and determined.

McGurk was reaching up to the handle of the

van's back door. The man lunged forward, and before McGurk knew what had happened his face was
turning a deep red, with the man's forearm locked
against his throat, squeezing it between the arm
and the man's chest.

"Got 'em!" said Brains, not realizing what was
going on as he came hurrying around from the
front, holding up the keys.

"Hand them over—quick!" snarled the man. "Or
your friend here gets his neck snapped!"

"Do—uh—like he—uh—says!" gasped McGurk, his eyes popping.

(Cowardly? No. Common sense? Yes. As McGurk said later, he knew Willie was on his way for help.)

"Thanks!" growled the man, snatching the keys with his free hand. He used them to rap on the door. "Open up, Mac! It's me!"

With a rattle, the door swung open. It was dim in there, but not so dark as to conceal the small huddled figure of Mari in a far corner.

"Be careful, Chief McGurk!" she said. "He has gun!"

There was no need to warn McGurk. He was still in the headlock, still purply red in the face, eyes bulging. And the gun was already in Mac's hand.

"What—?"

"Skip the questions! Grab these keys, gimme the gun and get behind the wheel. I'll take care of these two. The boy's coming with us. We can't—"

"Hold it! Police!"

Never have I been so glad to hear Mr. Cassidy's voice—even though all the good humor had gone out of it.

He had drawn his gun. Willie was behind him, looking flushed.

"Come *on*, you up there! Lay that gun down on the floor! Slowly! With the fingertips!"

Mac was looking scared, already stooping to obey.

"Sure! Sure! I—we—"

"Don't be a jerk, Mac!" snarled the tall man. He gave McGurk's throat an extra squeeze and turned to Mr. Cassidy, holding our leader like a shield. "*You* put *your* gun down, copper! I've got this kid in a death hold. One move and he's a goner!"

Mr. Cassidy suddenly looked uncertain. He lowered his gun slightly.

"You, Mac," said the tall man, "look sharp and—"

But that was all he ever got to say at *that* time.

Because just then a very strange thing happened.

There was a horrible, blood-chilling, threatening yell, which I swear seemed to come from somewhere a few feet to the left of the man. Certainly that's where he turned *his* head, looking as startled as the rest of us.

But that was not all.

Out of the back of the van, something like a sixty-pound young tigress came hurtling forward in a tremendous spring—a spring that was redoubled in force when that hurtling body reached out and used the head of Mac, who was still stooping—as a pivot.

Then the small body—flying supersonic now—shot out, feet first.

Mari's feet were small. But with that force behind them they were like hammers. The two heels, close together, hit the tall man precisely at the back of his right ear and he went down like a bowling pin. Mari reached the ground—lightly, springily—at roughly the same time. McGurk was a sloppy second or two later. His was neither a dead drop nor a spring landing. More like a slump.

"Hey!" he gasped, clutching his throat. "He could have *killed* me, Officer Yoshimura!"

It was pure shock, of course. There he'd been for several minutes, expecting the life to be snuffed out of him by one jerk of the man's arm. No wonder he felt a little indignant.

"Not so, Chief McGurk!" said Mari, bending over him and smiling sympathetically, while Mr. Cassidy was putting the handcuffs on Mac. (The other guy was still out cold.) "I know a little karate and other martial arts. My brothers teach me. And I could see no way was this man's hold a death hold. Painful, perhaps. Killing, no."

"Wow!" said Wanda. "But that jump! Was that—?"

"Something I learned? Yes. But still not perfect." Mari sighed. "I think I was lucky. But it had to be tried."

Well, *I* think Mari was being too modest, but she still stuck to the good-luck story later, when McGurk was pleading with her to teach *us* karate and she refused, saying she was not proficient enough. Also that it could be dangerous for beginners and that she was really a little annoyed at having been forced to do what she always told the doll in her act she must *never* do.

Meantime, though, that afternoon, McGurk was more concerned with wrapping up the case. Rubbing his neck, he went up to where Mr. Cassidy was now kneeling beside the slowly reviving tall man, and said:

"Should I ask one of my officers to phone for assistance, Mr. Cassidy?"

"That would be a good idea, yes," said the policeman. "Although this fella won't be giving much trouble for a while."

"No," said McGurk. "But there could be other members of the gang. Maybe waiting in a nearby backup vehicle."

"Oh?" Mr. Cassidy looked up. "What makes you think that?"

"Because my science expert here would have recognized their voices if these had been the same two he heard on the phone. Right, Officer Bellingham?"

"Uh—well—" Then Brains must have caught something of McGurk's supreme self-confidence. He nodded firmly. "Right!"

And he was!

"Mac," said the tall man, looking straight at *me* with swimming eyes, still concussed, "go warn Arch and Peters we struck a little snag!"

"Sure!" I said softly, suddenly seeing *my* chance to shine. "Where are they, though?"

An annoyed look crossed those dazed eyes.

"You never remember anything, Mac! In back of the old burned-out motel on Route 22, you dope!"

Then he passed out again.

16 McGurk Has a Dream....

In fact there were six members of the gang altogether, all planning to share the three million dollars ransom they hoped to get.

Two more were collared half an hour later, behind the old motel. They were waiting in the green van that Wanda and Mari had spotted several days before. One of these men did have a strong Boston accent, according to Mr. Cassidy. So he was probably one of the men Brains had overheard. If everything had gone smoothly, they would have switched Mari into the green van and ditched the red one.

The remaining two gang members turned out to be the phony repairman and the man who'd been tailing the girls. They were caught in a remote farmhouse in Connecticut, waiting for the other four to arrive with the girl. Once they'd accomplished their original tasks they had left our neighborhood. Mr. Cassidy said this is often done in well-planned operations.

"The scouts—the guys who do the casing and fingering—take care to be long gone before the crime is perpetrated," said the policeman.

This operation turned out to have been even better planned than we'd realized, though.

The phony repairman had bugged the Community Hall *as well as* the Grieg house. Mr. Healey remembered letting him in two days earlier. This bugging was so that the flower men could listen in from their van on Friday afternoon and make any necessary last-minute changes. Which they did, of course— though without realizing that it gave rise to one of the clues that finally alerted McGurk.

Naturally, we didn't get to hear all these details right away. They came out over the next few weeks.

What happened *immediately* after the rescue was typical of Mari. Just before he took the flower men away, Mr. Cassidy told us to stay where we were and wait to be questioned by another officer. Well, Mari insisted on making good use of the waiting time.

"I must do my act," she said. "As promised."

And do it she did, and it was a great hit with those senior citizens. Some of them came up to her when she was through, wanting to know if she'd perform at other parties and functions.

Mari had to decline.

"Sorry!" she said. "I am only here another week."

And that's when we felt a kind of cloud come over us.

It was still there the next morning, when we met in McGurk's basement, and it wasn't even swept away by the two special announcements.

The first was made by Mari. It was to say that her parents had called that morning.

"They say they will be coming here later today. They would like to give special thanks to my new friends."

The second announcement was made by McGurk. It was to say that he was canceling the exams.

"I've decided it wouldn't be fair to give any of you a higher rank than the others. You all did so good in this case"—(we all beamed with pleasure and relief)—"and you all did so *bad*!"

Our faces dropped.

"I mean, okay," McGurk went on. "Officer Bellingham uncovered the plot. Officer Grieg gave us valuable support in getting us installed at the scene of the crime. Officer Sandowsky spotted the really vital clues—the wrong perfume on the roses and the snuff. And Officer Rockaway had the brainwave and presence of mind that helped the police collar the other men as fast as they did."

Our faces were beginning to brighten again. He soon put a stop to *that*.

"*But*," he said, "not one of you was smart enough to read those early clues correctly! If you had, it would all have been cleared up days ago. As it was, we nearly allowed Mari to be snatched from under our noses!"

"All that goes for you, too, McGurk!" said Brains.

"Yeah! But I did read them correctly in the end!"

"What about Mari?" said Wanda. "Temporary Trainee Officer Yoshimura. How does *she* rate in all this?"

"*She* didn't realize what was happening, either,"

said McGurk. "Not until it was nearly too late."

Mari hung her head. Then lifted it when McGurk continued:

"But she did just fine, all the same. Spotting some of those early clues. And that *last* move—wow!" McGurk looked sideways at Mari. "You *sure* you can't teach us some of that stuff, Officer Yoshimura?"

"Sorry, Chief McGurk!"

Mari shook her head firmly.

McGurk nodded—and sighed.

"Anyway, there's one thing you *did* earn." He turned. "Officer Rockaway, I want you to type out a new ID card. Not Honorary Member. Not Temporary. Not Trainee. A regular membership card, please."

"Just like *ours*?"

"Exactly." McGurk turned to Mari and put out his hand. "Welcome aboard, *permanent* Officer Yoshimura!"

"Oh, thank you, thank you, thank you!"

I thought Mari was going to shake his arm off. Willie, Brains and Wanda all started to congratulate her.

I hated to interrupt. I was as pleased as any of them. But when it comes to words I do like to be strictly accurate.

"But, McGurk," I said. "How can Mari be anything *but* temporary? She goes back to Japan in a week."

Then McGurk leaned back. A big, blissful, dreamy smile spread over his face and a glazed look slid over his half-closed eyes.

"I know that, Officer Rockaway. But she still gets to keep her permanent active membership. How? As the McGurk Organization's official representative in Japan, that's how! With a branch office in Osaka." He looked around, still blissful. "This could be the start of a new phase in the Organization's history, men! An expanding, worldwide Organization, with members in every country. And . . . and . . . well. . . ."

Awed by his own dream, McGurk fell silent. So did we all.

Then Wanda glanced uneasily at Mari.

"I think you should know, McGurk, that there *is* just a chance that Mari might be staying in this country."

"Huh?"

"Yes." Wanda sounded wistful. "If Mr. Yoshimura does decide to open a factory here. They'd be buying a house and—"

"Then I will go to school here," said Mari.

"I mean, I hate to spoil your dream, McGurk," said Wanda (looking like nothing could please her more). "But it might be *years* before Mari goes back to Japan."

McGurk was frowning slightly. Then he shrugged.

"So what? It'll give her that much longer to study my methods and make a better job of the new office when she does open it up."

Then, to show he meant to carry on business as usual in the meantime, he gave his head a brisk shake and turned to me.

"Before you start on Mari's ID card, I want you to add a couple of words to the notice on the door."

I'd been wondering when he'd get around to this. After every case, he likes to brag about our latest achievement by including it on the list. By now we have a notice like a kite with a yard-long tail— starting with "Mysteries Solved" and going on to say things like "Missing Persons Found," "Persons Protected" and "Bank Robbers Busted."

"What do you suggest this time?" I asked.

He told me. And I have to admit it wasn't bad.

So now at the end of the notice there is this:

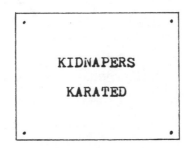

KIDNAPERS

KARATED